THE CHRISTMAS NOVELS
OF ANNE PERRY

A Christmas Journey

A Christmas Visitor

A Christmas Guest

A Christmas Secret

A Christmas Beginning

A Christmas Grace

A Christmas Promise

A Christmas Odyssey

A Christmas Homecoming

A Christmas Garland

A Christmas Hope

A New York Christmas

A Christmas Escape

A Christmas Message

A Christmas Return

A Christmas Revelation

A Christmas Gathering

A Christmas Resolution

A Christmas Legacy

A Christmas Deliverance

A Christmas Vanishing

A Christmas Vanishing

A Christmas Vanishing

A Novel

Anne Perry

BALLANTINE BOOKS · NEW YORK

Copyright © 2023 by Anne Perry

Published in the United States by Ballantine Books, an imprint of Random House, a division of Penguin Random House LLC, New York.

BALLANTINE is a registered trademark and the colophon is a trademark of Penguin Random House LLC.

Hardback ISBN 978-0-593-35918-1
Ebook ISBN 978-0-593-35919-8

Printed in the United States of America on acid-free paper

randomhousebooks.com

1st Printing

First Edition

Interior art credit: sangidan © Adobe Stock Photos

To Alice Romano
for her friendship

A Christmas Vanishing

*M*ariah Ellison was very comfortable in her window seat on the train, watching the countryside pass by. Winter in London was miserable. Everything was cold and gray. The ice-laden east wind scoured the pavements and funneled down the open streets. People hurried by, heads down against the icy, stinging sleet. Most of the time Mariah stayed at home and built up the fire in the sitting room of her small house in Kensington.

Out here in the countryside it was different. There was a wide sky with huge patches of blue. The air sparkled. The train passed villages where the trails of smoke were almost instantly blown away from chimneys and dissolved into the air. Here and there, the wind-facing slopes of the hills were white with the first snow. Lower down lay dark, plowed earth, like giant lengths of corduroy draped over the land, all ridges precisely even. They would soon be misted over with a veil of green, when the winter wheat first showed. It was one of the few good certainties of life.

The future was an unknown land ahead, a new century, and certainly a new king. Victoria was old, and she looked as tired as she must feel. It could not be long now. Would things change slowly? Mariah thought not. Everyone had been waiting too long. The new ideas that had been on the horizon all this time would burst forth. She recognized that inventions such as the automobile were useful. So were a dozen other things. It was the ideas, the casting away of old values, that troubled her. But what frightened her was that, now in her eighties, she felt increasingly old and fragile . . . and vulnerable.

And now she was revisiting the past, a thing she very rarely did, for many reasons. In truth, there was little in her past that she wished to remember. But Sadie Alsop had written to her from the village of St. Helens in Dorset, inviting her to spend Christmas with Sadie and her husband, Barton Alsop.

Sadie and Mariah had been friends for decades. Mariah had even lived in St. Helens for a short while. She liked the place, but, for other reasons, it was a time she did not remember with any clarity, nor did she wish to. However, Sadie's friendship stood out, and at one time or another Mariah had gone back to visit. In all these years of her widowhood, she had been free to go wherever she pleased. And now it was time to see Sadie again.

It was a surprise, this invitation from Sadie. The last time they had parted, about twenty years previously, it had not been with good feelings. Mariah could no longer remember the precise details of the quarrel, but she assumed it was due to her own ill temper. She had changed since then. She had at last faced her demons, the memories of her unhappy marriage and the person she had become because of it that had caused her pain and such a crushing self-loathing that it still hurt. Probably, it always would. But she had discovered that it was better to face the pain than to look away. If she denied it, every dark memory would become monstrous.

At this moment, if she was being honest, she had to accept that she had nowhere else to go, which was entirely her own doing. Her daughter-in-law and grandchildren all had their own seasonal arrangements, and she had not been included.

But that was not the reason why she was sitting here, rattling through the countryside, less than a week before Christmas. It was because she had sensed that Sadie's letter was a plea for Mariah's help. She did not know why, or with what, exactly. They had been friends half a lifetime ago, and kept in touch now and then. Only recently had their communication diminished to no more than an exchange of cards once or twice a year. Sadie must be well into her seventies by now. For heaven's sake, Mariah was over eighty! Exactly how much over she preferred to recall only vaguely.

A little while ago, Mariah would have declined this invitation. Too much trouble for no good reason. And why rake over the details of old grudges, their causes long forgotten? Mariah had been self-righteous, she now acknowledged. It was time to forget it, wipe it out. Her remaining life was too short to be squandered that way. She tired easily, she ached in all sorts of places, and sometimes she lost her balance—she had enough to contend with, and yet she was making an effort.

Mariah had been forced to see herself as others saw her, and it was painful. Not only had she been ill-tempered, but she had been self-absorbed and had frequently seen only the worst in people. She realized now that she had been a coward, too fearful to change—until recently.

She thought back to Sadie's letter. At first, it had read like a simple invitation to an old friend to visit for Christmas. But when she had read on, she had sensed fear. Even more than that, an undercurrent of despair.

She brought back to mind all she could remember of Sadie. They had liked each other, although they were different in so many ways, physically as well as in character. Mariah was short, and in later years, undeniably heavy. Her hair was thick, even though now it was white, but she was still handsome. Her eyes were dark, as was her complexion. Sadie was taller, slender, fair-haired, and always graceful. Mariah remembered that Sadie smiled a lot, making light of troubles. She was often amused by things that bothered other people.

There was little of that humor in her current letter. In fact, reading it the third time, Mariah could not escape the fact that it was a cry for help. Of course, Sadie did not say so outright. She would never do that, because it would betray the fact that something important had slipped out of her control. In spite of herself, Mariah smiled as memories rushed in, pleasant memories. The two of them had catered parties together, with Sadie never mentioning how many people were coming. She acted as if she were always in command. She baked the lightest sponge cakes, and had an infinite variety of ways to decorate them, or alter the flavor with fruit, cream, nuts, or icing. She knew how to bake flaky pastry. "Cold hands," she would say, when asked. "Cold hands, warm heart for light pastry."

Recalling this, Mariah found herself smiling.

She glanced up and saw that the woman seated opposite her, traveling backward, was watching Mariah as she sat there smiling to herself, apparently at nothing.

There were more memories going back to the 1850s

7

and longer, and now here she was, looking at the end of the century. Why did she feel as if they were all sitting in a boat without an engine and racing along the river, driven by wind and current, toward a giant waterfall dropping off the cliff into—what? No one knew.

She asked herself: *What did you do with your life?* but then quickly forced the question and its answers out of her mind. Surely, it was a good thing that in Sadie's time of . . . what, trouble? difficulties? indecision? whatever it was, she had turned to Mariah again, giving her the opportunity to heal some old wounds.

But why had Sadie asked *her* to come? Because she was an outsider to the village? Because, for all her faults, which were many, she was brave and stood up to people? Was that true? Yes, at times it was. Perhaps it wasn't courage so much as it was anger, even outrage, if she saw injustice, but even that was courage of a sort. Generosity could call it that. To those less inclined, it was a quick, hot temper and little tolerance for people who prevaricated because they did not want to commit themselves to an opinion. Or worse, they did not have one.

The train was slowing down. Not only could she see it, she could hear it in the rhythmic clanking every time they passed a joint in the rails. They must be pulling into St. Helens. Heaven knew, they had stopped at every other village since London! But that was the only way to get to the small places. And St. Helens was certainly small. One high street and half a dozen others with shops of all sorts, necessary and unnecessary, and then a wider web of roads out into the countryside. Two churches: St. Helens, which was of course Anglican, and another of some sort of nonconformist religion. And one school.

She recalled that there had been no duck pond on the village green, and still thought this was a mistake. She remembered how she and Sadie had argued about it. Looking back, she realized that the disagreement was not about a duck pond, but about who was right.

The train was slowing even more. In another minute they would reach the station. Then it would be too late to change her mind and turn back. Stuff and nonsense! It was too late when she had said she would come. She had frequently expressed her utter contempt for those who made promises and broke them. She could not afford to be one of them.

The train came to a stop. It was time to ask the porter to lift down her bags from the rack, thank him, and go carefully down the steps to the platform.

She was here. The sign on the platform said "St. Helens." There was no more daydreaming about it, recalling memories and evading the present.

About a half-dozen people got off the train. There was only one porter, and Mariah had two cases she could not lift, let alone carry. She should have brought less. Too late now.

She told the porter she required a cab, and he disappeared to find one for her. The train had actually pulled out of the station when he arrived back. He had been gone perhaps less than five minutes, but the bitter cold made it feel longer. As she stood there, she wondered if they chose windy places to build these stations on purpose. Or perhaps it was cheaper to buy land for the railway where nobody wanted to live.

The porter picked up both of Mariah's cases and set off down the platform toward the exit. Mariah followed him briskly, her heels clacking on the stone.

A horse-drawn buggy, open to the elements, was waiting by the verge. Thank heaven she had not far to go. She would be a solid block of ice if it were more than a mile or two.

"Thank you," she said to the porter, and gave him sixpence. It was quite a good tip.

The ride down the road brought memories crowding back. The bare trees by the sides seemed smaller than she remembered. They should have been wider, and

taller. They were twenty years older, at least! But then
the past was often smaller than one recalled. The hedge
alongside the road was the same tangle of bushes. She
hoped it still had wild roses growing in it, but she would
not be here to find out. Perhaps that was just as well.
Leave the past where it was! She shivered, and pulled
her coat more tightly round her. At least it was not rain-
ing.

They were into the village now. The houses looked
just as they had always been. Neat gardens, all of them
ready for awakening, eager for the spring. Hedges were
clipped. Only the laurel leaves were green, and the pine
trees, of course. Rosebushes were bare thorny sticks in
the ground, but pruned, well cared for. In the summer
they would reappear, stronger than before.

They went past the village green, then the driver
pulled the horse to a stop. "Here yer are, ma'am," he announced cheerfully. "I'll get them cases for yer."

She watched him as he climbed down, and then came
to help her. She was glad of his assistance, and thanked
him. She paid the fare and then walked up the path.
Her throat was tight. What was Sadie going to ask of
her? Would she measure up to the task? Had Sadie already asked all her friends in the neighborhood, and
had come to Mariah only as a last resort?

She continued up the well-kept path and rang the

doorbell, giving the rope a sharp pull. She could hear it ringing somewhere in the house.

There was no answer.

She waited. It was surprisingly cold on the step. The wind felt as if it were directed at her personally. She pulled the rope again, but harder. This was absurd. Sadie must be expecting her. After all, she had invited her, and had taken the trouble to look up the times of the trains and recommend which one would be best.

She was reaching to pull the bell a third time when the door opened. Barton Alsop stood just inside, staring at her. Mariah remembered him being bigger than he looked now, but he was still imposing, and still handsome. He had not lost much of his hair, although it was graying, as were his eyebrows. He was clean shaven now. He used to wear a mustache. This was an improvement.

"Yes?" he said sharply. It was a question that suggested not only *what do you want?* but also *who the hell are you?*

Mariah was not pleased to have to explain herself. Had Sadie not told him that she was coming? How should she address him? She had forgotten. Was he Barton, or was he Mr. Alsop?

It was apparent that he did not recognize her. The

driver standing behind her with her cases must surely indicate to him that she expected to stay here. Or, perhaps, somewhere near here. But Sadie had quite definitely said, "Stay with us."

Barton Alsop took a deep breath.

"Mariah Ellison," Mariah said. "We have known each other on and off for fifty years. Sadie invited me to stay over Christmas. And she sent me the train timetables, so she knows when I should arrive." She stopped. The look on his face would stop anyone.

They stared at each other in freezing silence. There was no sound but that of the wind chasing dry leaves along the pavement.

"Mr. Alsop!" Mariah's voice was sharp.

"You can't stay here," he said abruptly. "Sadie isn't here."

"When will she be back?" Mariah demanded. "I can't stand here on the doorstep all afternoon!"

His face was pale, his skin tight, as if it were stretched over his bones. "You can stand here as long as you like," he snapped. "Sadie isn't here. She's gone. I don't know if she's ever coming back. You'll freeze out there, but you can't come in. It isn't decent, apart from anything else. The pub has a room above the bar if you don't know anyone else. But I can't help you." And with that he stepped backward into the hall and slammed the door.

Mariah stumbled along the path in shock, back to the gate and the waiting cab. The driver followed behind with her bags. After he had assisted her into the seat, he climbed down and stowed her bags again. His face looked troubled.

"You all right, ma'am?" he asked with concern. "He didn't—" He stopped. Clearly, he did not know what to say next.

"Thank you." She swallowed, momentarily stuck for words.

"I know Mrs. Alsop," the driver said. "She's a nice lady. Is she all right?"

"I don't know," Mariah admitted. "It was . . . It doesn't make any sense. She invited me." Why was she explaining to a driver? Because he was the only one listening. "I have to find . . ." She trailed off. Find someone to make sense of what had happened? Someone to put her up for the night, at least?

"Somewhere to sit down and have a hot cup o' tea?" the driver suggested. "You have friends here, in St. Helens, I reckon, as I've seen you before, a while back."

That at least made sense. "Yes. I've been here. Quite a long time ago now." She had no idea where else to go, but she could not stay here in the street, in front of a house where she was clearly not welcome. "Thank you," she accepted. "I think if you take me to Mrs. Spears's house, she might know what's happened. And where Mrs. Alsop is." She gave a tiny shrug, no more than a gesture. She felt exhausted. And bruised. She had done nothing except walk along platforms and sit in trains all day. The more Mariah thought about Sadie's absence, the more concerned she became.

"Right, ma'am." The driver nodded, and he drove away. He did not need to be told where the Spearses lived, which was a good thing, because Mariah could remember that it was on Bedford Street, but had forgotten what number.

The village was peaceful, just as she remembered it. Hardly any sound other than the horse's hoofs, and the hiss of wheels in the slush from earlier snowfalls. A boy went by on a bicycle, ringing its bell cheerfully.

Along the high street Mariah recognized the same shop fronts she had always known, and a few new ones. The towering oak on the main road junction was ancient, its gnarled roots like snakes breaking the acorn-strewn ground in its shade. An old man was roasting chestnuts over a brazier beneath it. Was he one of the men who had been doing that, and in the same place, fifty years ago, when Mariah first came here? He looked the same, but perhaps memory painted him that way.

They passed the village green. It was neatly mown around the paths that crossed it. The few trees looked, from the way the branches grew, like flowering cherry. There used to be swathes of daffodils in March and April, but there was still no village pond. They should have made one, to have ducks in it and to give children the joy of feeding them.

The carriage turned from the meandering Main Street into the best residential area, a matter of four or five streets, with the church of St. Helens in the center.

"They have a forsythia bush in the front garden," Mariah said to the driver. "Or at least they used to have." She listened to herself and decided that she sounded idiotic. This was awful. If she were not so thrown off balance and worried about Sadie, she would have felt profoundly ridiculous. And here she was, dependent on this cabdriver. It meant she had lost control of events.

"I remember that, ma'am." The driver's voice broke through her thoughts. "I know just where the house is. Take you straight there, don't you worry."

There was only one safe and suitable answer. "Thank you." She meant it sincerely.

The driver was as good as his word. Five minutes later they drew up in front of the house, with the lawn before it and a seven-foot-high bare forsythia bush, which was now a small tree that would be ablaze with flowers in the early spring.

"Thank you," Mariah said again, for a moment almost choked with relief. "Yes, thank you." She relaxed as she watched him climb down onto the pavement and walk up the pathway to the front door. He knocked. The door opened at once and a man stood just inside. He was slender and his hair flopped loosely over his brow. It was light gray, as if it had once been light brown. The lines on his face were deep, but they spoke of an easy smile.

Mariah recognized John Spears. She felt the years slip away, and wished those years had been different. Her years, that is, filled as they were with humiliation, anger, and regret. Did she really win against it? Or was she trying now to convince herself that it was all dealt with?

The driver was talking to John, who had not given the gig and its passenger more than a glance. Now he looked past the driver and directly at Mariah. He gave the driver a quick pat on the arm, then walked past him and down the path to the pavement. He stopped a few feet from Mariah. "How are you?" he asked. "You must be tired, coming all the way from London, and then to find this." He smiled very slightly. "I didn't know you were coming, or I'd have tried to warn you."

Mariah was at first warmed by his pleasantness, but it did not explain anything. "Warn me? Do you know where Sadie has gone to? She invited me and knew I was coming today. She even looked up the trains to save me having to do it. It must have been very urgent for her to go away at this time. You don't invite someone to stay with you, and then disappear!" She was aware how sharp her voice sounded, as if she were somehow accusing John of something. She closed her eyes for a moment, and took a deep breath. "I'm sorry." She was unused to apologizing.

"It's not your fault," John said quickly. "Nobody knows where Sadie went, or why, or whether she will be back tonight. At least nobody will admit to it. It is a trifle worrying. Why don't you ask the driver to carry your cases to our front porch, and you can come in and have a rest, a cup of tea, warm you up, while we consider what is to be done?"

Mariah suddenly realized how tired she was, even though she had been sitting a great deal of the time. But sitting upright in a train seat is not relaxing at all.

The best one could say for it was that it was better than standing. She had dared not drift off to sleep lest she end up somewhere on the south coast. "Thank you," she accepted. "I'm not sure what to do, until I . . ." How should she finish the sentence? There were too many ifs. If Sadie came back? If she sent a message with instructions? If she asked Mariah to join her somewhere else? But why on earth should she do that? Sadie had lived in or around St. Helens most of her life.

John gave instructions to the cabdriver, although Mariah insisted on paying him herself, and giving him a good tip for his kindness. She told him so, to his surprise, and hers, too! She was not used to thanking service people for doing what she considered was their job.

With the suitcases in the house and the driver gone, John led the way across the hall, calling out to his wife. "Annabel! Annabel. We have a visitor. How about tea? It's just the right time."

Annabel appeared in the sitting-room doorway. She, too, looked exactly as Mariah remembered her, only older, more faded than the striking woman she had been two decades or more ago. She was still tall, but thicker at the waist, which was not surprising, seeing that she was well into her seventies. Mariah knew that those she had been acquainted with here must be mostly into their seventies or, like Mariah herself, their eighties. To pretend the years had not passed was absurd.

Annabel looked Mariah up and down. "Well, my dear, how are you?" she said warmly.

She only ever called Mariah "my dear" when John was around. It had happened so regularly; Mariah should have remembered that. But she could play the same game, and just as well, if she chose. "Very well, thank you," she said with more pleasure than she felt. "And I see that you are, too. You look just the same as the last time I was here, which was ages ago." That was a lie. All those passing years were somehow written in Annabel's face and the wispy hair, grayer than before, the slightly rheumatic hands, larger-knuckled than they used to be. Mariah knew exactly what to look for, because age was evident in her own face and hands as well. But unlike Annabel's hair, her own had lost none of its weight or luster.

"Thank you." Annabel smiled sweetly. "It must be the country air."

Mariah lived in London, with its dirt, noise, and fog, and beneath it a burning vitality, but not the country, by anyone's standards. "I suppose you trade one thing for another," she said lightly. "In London, there are so many things to occupy the mind and feed the imagination. It is said that if you stand in Piccadilly Circus long enough you will see everyone in the world who is anyone at all." Let her find some answer to that!

John sneezed. It was probably laughter, quickly smothered.

You know on which side your bread is buttered, Mariah thought.

"I suppose if you live there, you would agree with them, if only for good manners' sake." Annabel smiled coolly as she looked Mariah up and down. "You look totally exhausted. You must have a cup of tea, and something to eat while we think what we can do to help you. I wish we could offer to put you up, but I'm afraid we simply haven't the room. But do come in and sit down. It will do you good, and you are blue with cold!" She stepped backward as if to make room for Mariah, who was still standing in the middle of the hall.

John touched Mariah's shoulder lightly. "May I take your coat?"

"Of course," Annabel answered before Mariah could draw breath. "Or you won't feel the benefit of it when you leave."

Mariah had to accept, but she sensed that Annabel's words were intended to sting, and she could not think of an answer to them. She allowed John to take the coat,

21

and turned around to follow Annabel into the large, warm sitting room. It was as if time had stood still. It looked exactly the same as when she had last been here twenty years ago. The armchairs were the same, sagging a little but extremely comfortable, and upholstered with the same rose-patterned chintz fabric as the curtains. She noticed that one chair had been replaced, but upholstered with such a simple design: roses all over, rose shades of pinks and reds. It blended in perfectly. "I see you have kept the same chairs!" she said with pleasure. "I am glad. It is such a pretty design." She walked over to the one placed beside the fire and sat down. "I remember, you always were so clever with patterns." That was a lie, too, but Annabel could hardly deny it.

John walked in and sat in the chair across from Mariah, on the other side of the fire, but only after drawing up a third for Annabel.

Annabel disappeared from the room, and John sat back, crossing his legs and appearing very comfortable.

"How is your family?" he asked. "You have a son, and granddaughters, I believe. I hope they're well?"

Suddenly, the gap in years since she had been here yawned wide. Indeed, even a polite inquiry reminded her how long it was. "I'm afraid my son died," she said, her voice level and without self-pity. It had never ceased to hurt, but acceptance made it tolerable. "My daughter-in-law remarried." She remembered this sharply. The scandal had confounded her. Then she had realized how Caroline was liberated, if she could accept it. Edward had been a strict man, but kind. Unimaginative. Was that her fault? Possibly. She had, at one time, thought imagination led to all kinds of time wasted on futile ideas, impractical and self-indulgent. It was a wicked thought. Thank the Lord it had not affected Caroline's decision one whisker. But it might have hurt all the same.

John Spears looked at her as he waited for her to continue. Nice manners, or was he really interested? As far as she could recall from previous visits, nothing very much ever happened in St. Helens, but an awful lot was imagined, repeated, and magnified in the telling. She knew that from Sadie's infrequent letters.

She glanced at John and gave a little smile. She might as well enjoy herself. Things could hardly get worse! "She married an actor," she shared.

John looked confused. "I beg your pardon?"

"An actor," Mariah repeated. "You no doubt have seen them on the stage?"

"You mean, in a musical?" Now he looked nonplussed.

"I don't believe so. Rather more Shakespeare. Oscar

23

Wilde, on the lighter side." Had she gone too far? Oscar Wilde's recent disgrace was still spoken of in soft tones, salaciously, or sympathetically. Some people could not help liking the man, and certainly admiring his wit. Others did not like or understand him, and hated him for disturbing their rigid ideas. Mariah wanted to be contrary to both, but ended up siding with Wilde. Wit, real wit, especially of the spiky sort that made one think, always pleased her. It enraged some people terribly when she quoted Wilde and affected not to know what all the fuss was about when told of his offense. She could tell them that many whom they accepted without question were guilty of far more vile deeds. But that door was locked and bricked up in her mind. She took a deep breath. She might well find herself on the train back to London tomorrow morning. "In fact, Joshua reminds me of you. In his manner, that is, his— kindness."

There was utter silence in the room. The coal settled a little in the fireplace and sent up a bright shower of sparks.

"Joshua? What an unusual name," John remarked. "Biblical?"

"I believe he is Jewish," Mariah answered, still meeting his eyes steadily.

"And you say you like him?" he asked, as if assuring himself they were still on the same subject.

Mariah burned the final bridge. "Yes, I did. I still do. Caroline goes all over the world with him, and is enjoying her life enormously."

He sat staring at her, as if waiting for the inevitable conclusion.

"And, of course, my second granddaughter married a policeman," she continued. "Very happily. And her sister married a member of Parliament. You could think what you please about that, but I rather like the man."

"The policeman, or the member of Parliament?" he asked, not quite keeping the sudden amusement out of his voice.

Mariah could imagine him sitting up in bed beside Annabel, who would be wearing her high-necked pink nightdress, hand to her throat in assumed horror. She would probably be green with envy at the scandal of it all.

Shaking her head, Mariah responded, "Dreadful cases he's worked on. You'd be surprised how many of them involve members of the highest society."

He stared at her for seconds. She knew he was deciding how much of this to believe.

"I learn from the press," Mariah said with a slight

25

smile. "I never read newspapers when Edward was alive, but now I do as I please."

John relaxed a little, settling deeper into his chair and smiling. "That I believe without hesitation."

Mariah was spared the necessity of replying by the return of Annabel with the tea trolley. It still had one wonky wheel, which she remembered from years ago.

There was tea in a large pot, covered over by a cozy that vaguely resembled a human head. But it served its purpose. It was undoubtedly a gift from someone, made with two left hands, to judge by the workmanship. Perhaps a child? Such things were uniquely precious, woven into one's life with a memory, and irreplaceable. It showed a softer side of Annabel than Mariah had seen before. She had one or two such items herself, made by her granddaughters, long ago.

There were several buttered scones on a dish, and a bowl of thick raspberry jam, and another of clotted cream. One could forgive a lot in a woman who would serve such a tea.

"Wonderful!" Mariah said sincerely. "I see you have lost none of your art. Suddenly, I am ravenous."

"Ham sandwich," Annabel offered. "It's late for cucumbers, even from the greenhouse. But hard-boiled eggs, with a little curry powder, are always good. Our younger son is out in India. Did John tell you? The other one is in Africa. But Africa has so many countries, and my memory is unreliable so I forget their names. He sent us delightful sketches, with a little watercolor highlighting things. I never grasp how some people know exactly what to put in and what to leave out."

"I think a lot of the world could be summed up that way," John observed with a slightly wry smile.

"The art of conversation certainly could," Mariah agreed, with a fraction too much fervor.

Annabel ignored her husband and turned to Mariah. "I have been avoiding your present unfortunate situation. I suppose Barton was too upset to send you a telegram telling you not to come—"

"He said that he didn't even know Sadie had invited me," Mariah cut across her. "So, he was taken completely by surprise, finding me on the doorstep."

"He must've forgotten," Annabel answered. "You know he has a terrible memory."

"You don't forget that someone is coming to stay with you," Mariah argued straight back. "There is clean linen in the spare bedroom, more food of the sort you serve to guests. Furniture rearrangements, all the best things on show. Don't tell me you would not notice that!"

"I certainly would," said John.

"Really, John!" Annabel said critically. "That's hardly important when Sadie herself is gone! So where is she? What on earth has she done?"

Mariah looked from one of them to the other. Annabel was angered and, to a degree, worried. John was still unwilling to admit there was any cause for concern. But in spite of the roaring fire, the comfortable chair, and the scones and jam and clotted cream, Mariah was fearful. "Has Sadie become so forgetful that she could be lost?" she asked. "Has Barton notified the police? No one in their right mind would spend the night outside, wandering around in this weather! What has he done to find her?" She took a shaky breath, as the reality of it forced itself to the front of her mind. "She could be lying in a ditch somewhere! If she fell, and—"

"Not at all!" Annabel dismissed the idea. "She's just being melodramatic! She's often getting little digs in at Barton. It's her way of getting his attention. If you lived here, instead of visiting every few decades, or were a little sharper in your observation, you would know that."

Mariah raised her eyebrows. "She often disappears in the middle of winter, and is gone all night, when she's expecting guests?" she said incredulously. "Then she should see a doctor. I suppose you have asked the doctor? And the police? You do still have a doctor in the village, don't you?"

"No," said Annabel. "Dr. Harris died. He was almost ninety, you know. There's quite a good doctor in Bridgetown and, of course, it's only a few miles away. Ten minutes by train. He comes here once or twice a week or so. Really, Sadie's just looking for attention, as usual. I'm only sorry she's chosen to do it at your expense. But she always had a selfish streak running through her."

"Annabel, that's a little harsh," John said, a faint color in his cheeks. Was he embarrassed for her? "Sadie exaggerates a bit—we all know that—but this is different. She's disappeared, and no one knows where she is. She hasn't been seen since yesterday morning."

"You're the one exaggerating, John," said Annabel with a note of scorn. "Playing into her hands. She spent a night away from home. Which was naturally going to draw attention, because poor Barton can hardly hide it, since Mariah was coming. Any woman could see through that!" She raised her eyebrows. "I'm surprised you still can't. She's a bit forgetful, now and then. Many of us are, as we get older, as you know yourself. But she wouldn't forget that Mariah was coming. She just wants to make as big a noise as she can. Selfish. I'm sorry, but that's true." She turned round and stared at Mariah. "Isn't it? Where are you going to sleep? You can't go back tonight, and I doubt you want to book the room at the pub!"

"She won't have to," John cut in before Mariah could draw breath to reply.

"John, we haven't got room for her!" Annabel snapped.

"Gwendolyn would be only too pleased to have her, as long as necessary," he said, equally sharply.

"I had not thought of my sister," Annabel admitted. "She is not prepared for guests, and as you may remember, she is hardly organized. She is still alone, you know? She never married. We did our best to introduce her to suitable men, but as time passed it became more and more difficult."

A sharp retort was on Mariah's lips, but she could not afford to voice it. She hated being constrained from speaking her mind, but she was at Annabel's mercy. "I'm sure you did your best," she said, as civilly as she could. "Perhaps Sadie will come home tonight."

"I'll send word for the cab," said John. "And I'll come with you, just to see that Gwendolyn can accommodate you, and that she is in."

"Where else would she be but at home, at this time in the afternoon?" said Annabel. "It's dusk, for heaven's sake, of the shortest day of the year." She waited, as if to see if her husband would argue, but he did not.

"Thank you," Mariah said. "It would help if Gwendolyn would accept me until I find out what may have happened to Sadie. I admit, I'm now quite concerned about her."

"Perhaps I'll go to Gwendolyn's now and let her know you're coming," said John, rising to his feet.

Mariah felt color in her cheeks. That was a sharp reminder that she was already in their debt for her interruption of their afternoon. They had to stop their occupations, whatever they had been, even if it had been merely a short nap. And Annabel had made a particularly luxurious tea. "I will be happy to pay for the cab." She felt clumsy, and she was aware of sounding it, but she could not remain silent.

"Oh, really!" said Annabel. "The cost is a pittance."

John looked at Annabel, then turned to Mariah. "I don't think Annabel intended that to sound as rude as it was. If the whole enterprise, until you are settled and comfortable for the night, amounts to more than half a crown, I'll toss you for it." And without waiting for a reply, he went out into the hall, and a moment later they heard the door close behind him.

There was silence for a moment. Then Annabel was

offering a second cup of tea and another scone, and asking Mariah if she wished for more clotted cream.

*F*ifteen minutes later, John returned. He was speaking to the driver as if they were old friends.

Mariah had always liked John, and now she remembered why.

He was clearly pleased with himself. "Gwendolyn is preparing your room," he said, "and she's delighted to have you as her guest."

After a quick goodbye to Annabel, Mariah followed John out to the buggy. It was the same horse-drawn cab that had taken her from the train first to Sadie's house, and then here, to Annabel's. John placed her bags in the back, got up beside the driver, and they were soon on the road.

It was dark now, and getting rapidly colder as night closed in. It wasn't like London, where the gas lamps burned warm, casting yellow light on all but the narrowest alleys.

Mariah glanced at the driver several times. He nodded to her pleasantly, but his face was unreadable. No doubt he knew a lot about people who had no idea they were being observed.

She wondered what he thought of her. A grumpy old woman in black who did not know where she wanted to be, and when she got there, was turned out again? Please heaven Gwendolyn was sincere in her willingness to take in a guest! Now that it was dark, the thought of having to book a room in the pub, directly above the bar, was dreadful. More than dreadful, it was a nightmare!

Could Annabel have accommodated her if she'd wished to, or was John just critical? They did not seem as much at ease with each other as she had remembered. Although she had to admit that Annabel was a great deal less clever than Mariah had once believed.

They rode in silence the rest of the way, which was something under a mile.

As they approached Gwendolyn's home, it was very clear that she was in. It seemed as if all the lights in the house were lit, and some of the windows had designs in colored transparent paper that gave them the illusion of stained glass. Mariah was surprised at herself by how it pleased her.

The horse stopped and the driver turned to John.

"I'll go and see if she's ready for us," John said as he

climbed down from the buggy, then walked up the pathway and knocked on the door.

A long minute ticked by, and another. Then the door opened and Gwendolyn Cooper stood there. Even from the seat of the cab, Mariah could see her broad smile, and she felt the stiffness leave her shoulders.

A moment passed, then Gwendolyn looked beyond John to the cab, and Mariah, still sitting there. Gwendolyn's smile became even wider. John turned round and started to walk back, but Gwendolyn passed him and stopped in front of Mariah. "Welcome! Welcome to St. Helens. I'm so sorry Sadie is still gone. Goodness knows why! Must have been an emergency of some sort. But her loss is my good luck. I'd love you to stay as long as you like. You have your luggage? Good. George will bring it in, won't you, George?" She turned for a moment to the driver.

Mariah let her breath out. It was ridiculous, but she had to blink away tears of relief. Gwendolyn was Annabel's younger sister, and had always been Mariah's favorite of the two. "Do you think so?" she asked. "That is, there's been some kind of emergency?" She could not keep the concern out of her voice. She realized how tired she was, how anxious from not knowing where she would be, at least for tonight. She had had no time alone, which was what she was so used to: time just to

34

breathe deeply and relax, not to have to think about deportment, or good manners.

Mariah entered the house and followed Gwendolyn upstairs. She hadn't noticed the driver or John transferring her cases, but they were in the spare room. The bed was already made up with fresh linen. "Lovely," she said, looking around the place.

"Come, let's go down and I'll prepare supper."

Minutes later, Mariah was seated in the warm kitchen whilst Gwendolyn found more vegetables to add to the stew they were going to share. As Gwendolyn prepared it, Mariah watched her hostess. The woman had not changed a lot in the years since Mariah had last seen her. Like her sister, Annabel, she was tall. Unlike Annabel, Gwendolyn was still slender. Her eyes were dark brown, her hair even darker, and now streaked with gray. It suited her. The woman who had once been stark and rather ordinary was now distinguished. The bones of her face were more defined, and age suited her.

Mariah found herself relaxing. She asked for a knife so she might help to slice the carrots.

"We will be a little late to eat," Gwendolyn apologized.

"That's fine with me." Mariah meant it profoundly. She felt welcome. She knew where she was going to sleep, for as long as necessary. And she was warm. Why was it so difficult to admit how grateful she was? It was not a situation she was used to.

"What do you think happened to Sadie?" she asked instead.

Gwendolyn looked more serious. "I'll bet she wasn't following the calendar and forgot this was the day you were coming. I never know what day it is if I don't check. Don't worry, you're really very welcome here. I haven't laid eyes on you for ages. Tell me what you've seen, what you've done! Above all, London is the center of the world, isn't it?"

Mariah drew in breath to deny it, then saw that Gwendolyn was laughing at her, happy laughter.

"Well, more than St. Helens is, anyway," she replied with a smile.

*M*ariah woke the next morning and found herself lying in Gwendolyn Cooper's guest bedroom, warm, comfortable, even welcome. But what had happened to Sadie? Was she simply careless? Forgetful? Had she planned to be at home to greet Mariah, but somehow had been unable to get back?

But if that was the case, why did Sadie's husband not expect her return, nor even know where it was she had gone? Was he telling the truth?

For years, Mariah had avoided truths she could not deal with. She was a past mistress when it came to ignoring things too painful to bear. But evil things, poisonous and destructive, can grow in the dark as well as in the light. Sometimes grow better. She should know that.

So, what had happened to Sadie?

She looked at her pocket watch. It was half past eight. Daylight, but gray, not penetrating the shadows. She got up, washed and dressed, and went downstairs to the kitchen, where the lamps were lit. Gwendolyn was standing by the stove and the table was set for breakfast.

"Ah! You're awake," Gwendolyn said with pleasure. "I hope you slept well. Were you warm enough?"

"Yes, thank you, very well indeed," Mariah replied with feeling. She was not normally an enthusiastic person. She thought of the hundreds of times she could have been appreciative, and had not been. It could not be helped now. But it could be changed. "I don't think I even turned over. I'm very grateful." Oddly enough, that had nothing to do with good manners. She meant it.

Gwendolyn gave her a quick smile. "That's my Christmas present, to have someone stay with me. We must have a tree, now that I have someone to share it with."

"I feel the same," Mariah answered, sitting down at the table. "I don't have one just for myself." This was perfectly true, but the first time she had admitted it. She wondered why Gwendolyn did not share the Christmas festivities with her sister and brother-in-law, as they lived in the same village.

"They still have ornaments at the village shop," Gwendolyn went on, taking the kettle off the hob. She warmed the teapot with a quick half cup or so of boiling water, then emptied it down the sink. She put a measure of tea leaves into the pot and then boiling water. "There now, five minutes and it will be fine. Boiled eggs, and then toast and marmalade?"

"Perfect," Mariah said sincerely.

Gwendolyn glanced at the kitchen clock. She took four eggs out of the saucepan and spooned them into the egg cups set on the table. The toast was already there, with the butter, and the marmalade in a big stone jar, clearly homemade. For the first time, Mariah realized how hungry she was.

The eggs were perfectly cooked, the toast was cool but still very fresh, and Mariah found the marmalade pleasantly tart. It was exactly what she would have made for herself, but it tasted far better when made by and shared with someone else.

They ate in silence for a few minutes, and then both started to speak at the same time. It was Gwendolyn who took up the subject that was on their minds.

"I hope you will feel welcome to stay here as long as you like," she said warmly. "I dare say that Sadie will be home today, but please know you are welcome here, and that it's no trouble to me at all."

"Thank you," Mariah accepted. She meant it with real gratitude, and a bit of relief. "But . . ." she began.

"I know," Gwendolyn said quickly. "We must find out what happened to her. This is not like her. She was looking forward to your coming. She said so several times."

"Is she absentminded?" Mariah asked. "We need the truth more than courtesy. I find myself obliged to make lists of things to buy because I don't always remember the best." That was true, but a reluctant admission.

Gwendolyn gave a quick smile. "For even the most obvious things. I get up and go to the kitchen, then forget what I came for!" She gave a little shrug.

"Is she?" Mariah persisted. "Absentminded, that is."

"No more than the rest of us," Gwendolyn answered.

"And she mentioned to us several times that you were coming, even the last time I saw her, which was only two days ago. I remember, I was at the grocer's, and she saw some ginger biscuits on the shelf. She bought a packet because she said you were fond of them."

That should have pleased Mariah. Instead, it frightened her. "We must find her," she said at once, her voice suddenly husky with unexpected emotion. The fewer friends you had, the more precious they became.

Gwendolyn shook her head. "But we have no idea where she has gone or, for that matter, why!"

"Then we must find out," Mariah replied. She was not making a lot of sense, and she knew it. She needed to think harder. "What if she's lost?" she continued. "Perhaps hurt. Or went to help somebody? Who does she know outside the village?"

Gwendolyn looked blank. "Nobody I can think of, certainly no one living so far that she wouldn't have come back before dusk. She was preparing for your arrival. It's not as if she forgot."

"Even if she forgot, she would have told Barton," Mariah pointed out.

Gwendolyn bit her lip. "Barton can be a bit bossy."

"Bossy," Mariah repeated, giving the word a heavier meaning, while trying not to borrow grief from her own memories. "Do you mean ordering her around? I never

40

knew Sadie to take any notice of that. Or do you mean bullying?" That, too, was an explanation that sprang from her own memories.

Gwendolyn looked down at her empty plate. "I don't know what I mean," she admitted. "I've never been married. I don't know whether it is normal. Annabel often tells me that John is a good man. But not everyone is so fortunate."

"No," Mariah agreed. "Not everyone tells the truth either, and why should they? Some grief tends to be endured alone. If you married someone, and they bullied you, or even struck you," she ignored Gwendolyn's startled look, "would you want the whole village to know it? Is there anyone at all that you would trust not to repeat it?"

"No," Gwendolyn said. "I would be embarrassed. But the village is so small. Wouldn't we know about it anyway? I mean . . ."

The thought entered Mariah's mind that their two different worlds were colliding. Gwendolyn's was one of solitary loneliness, of feeling excluded sometimes, cut out of things. Perhaps Gwendolyn did not realize how many women who seemed outwardly belonging, accepted, even cared for, were inwardly humiliated and in pain they could live with only by denying it.

"Then it is even more important that we find her,"

she said. "I would rather Barton Alsop thought me a nosy old busybody and find Sadie well, than not look for her and regret afterward that I cared more for what people thought of me than I did for Sadie's safety."

Gwendolyn bit her lip. "So would I! We can't all sit by our firesides at Christmas and ignore the fact that she is missing!"

"How long has she been gone?" Mariah asked.

"Since the day before yesterday, I believe," Gwendolyn replied. "I saw her at the shops in the morning, but not since then."

"What was she doing? Apart from getting the ginger biscuits."

"At the butcher's buying sausages. It was about half past ten."

"And Barton has said nothing?" Mariah pressed. "If they quarreled, it must be serious for her to leave without telling anyone." Mariah was thinking aloud. "How would she travel? Isn't the train the only way, if you don't have a gig, or a pony trap?"

"They haven't." Gwendolyn shook her head. "If they had, everyone would know."

"Of course," Mariah agreed. "Who saw her last, do we know that?"

Gwendolyn's expression became even more serious.

"It's the sort of thing we wouldn't like to ask. We only want to know other people's business to talk about it. And if it is something unpleasant, I suppose we don't want to know at all. In case we have to help." She winced, as if hearing the criticism in her voice, and promising herself not to be of this mind.

"But isn't everyone dying to know?" Mariah argued. "Unless they have had a complete change of character since I was here last."

"We like to know something that nobody else knows, and then hint at it," Gwendolyn agreed. "But if it's nasty, out of decency, we'll become bound to do something about it."

Mariah thought about that while she drank the last of her tea. "What if Sadie is hurt, lying somewhere that nobody knows about?"

"She'll be frozen to death," Gwendolyn whispered.

"Has anybody looked?"

"I don't think so. No one seems to think she's missing."

"Who would we report her missing to? There used to be a village constable."

Gwendolyn shook her head. "Not now. We could go to the nearest big town, but they would tell us to mind our own business! If Barton were to say she's gone to visit someone, they would believe him. And he has no obligation to explain to us. I know she invited you, and it's appallingly rude of her not to be here, but it's not a crime. Maybe she just took off in a temper." Gwendolyn took a deep breath. "She has a temper, you know. Didn't show it very often, and she'd be sorry afterward, but it was real."

Mariah did not answer that. It was just one more reality to be taken into account.

She thought of another possibility she did not like. "Do you think she did something wrong and ran away?"

"Wrong? Sadie?" Gwendolyn looked puzzled. "You mean really wrong?"

"Why not?" Mariah asked. "Haven't you ever done anything you were ashamed of and would rather other people didn't find out about it?" Dark memories raced around in her mind, cruel words she had said that could not be withdrawn. "I'm sorry," she said quietly. "But, unless she's back now, she's been gone two nights. This is serious."

Gwendolyn looked across the table at her. "I'm so glad you're here, Mariah. You always know what to do. And you were never a coward, not like the rest of us."

Mariah felt the heat burn up her face. If only Gwendolyn knew! Cowardice had been the primary sin in her

44

life. How different it might have been, had she been brave, and not too proud to admit anything was wrong. Or maybe not? But she could have tried. Perhaps then she wouldn't despise herself so much. "We will both be brave together," she stated, as if it were an agreed conclusion. "We will find out who saw Sadie last, where, if she said anything to them. And what she was wearing."

"Wearing?" Gwendolyn asked.

"If she was dressed warmly, with a scarf, and perhaps boots?" Mariah explained. "Or if she had leather gloves, and a hat, as if she was going to visit someone. This might help to answer our questions."

"Yes, of course." Gwendolyn's face lit with hope. "Maybe if we spoke with Barton, we might even find that she came home yesterday evening."

"An excellent idea," Mariah agreed.

They cleared the table and washed the dishes, and within a quarter of an hour, wrapped in winter coats and scarves, they were on the road to Sadie's house.

When they got there, Gwendolyn hung back a little, leaving Mariah to pull the doorbell.

She was about to reach for it for the third time when the door opened. Barton Alsop was a tall man and she was obliged to look up at him.

"Good morning," Mariah began. Her mouth was dry.

She took a deep breath. "I was hoping that Sadie might have returned."

"And then what?" he asked. "You can move in?"

"I would not be so rude," Mariah replied. "I am quite comfortable with Gwendolyn. I simply would like to know that Sadie is all right, not ill or injured."

His eyebrows rose. "For heaven's sake, Mrs. Ellison, of course she's all right. She's just had a lapse of memory. Perhaps she missed a train, or it was snowed in. It happens at this time of the year."

"How far has she gone, for heaven's sake, that the snow should be so deep?" Mariah demanded.

His face was dark with anger. "When she comes home, I shall ask her to go and visit you. That is, if you still are here. I'm sure she will come and apologize suitably."

Before Mariah could answer, he stepped back and closed the door.

Mariah was furious.

"Well!" Gwendolyn said decisively. "That answers one question, anyway!"

"And what is that?" Mariah demanded.

"He doesn't know where she is, and he's scared," Gwendolyn answered. "We must find her. She could be in trouble."

46

"What sort of trouble?" Mariah asked sharply. Not that she doubted Gwendolyn, but she needed some guidance or clue how to begin.

"I don't know," Gwendolyn admitted. "But he'd not be so worried about it if he knew."

"How do you know that?"

"He'd not be scared of us," Gwendolyn said reasonably. "It's something else. Anyone with sense is at least apprehensive about the unknown. Only somebody with no imagination at all takes it for granted that nothing bad can happen. And while Barton is an odd man sometimes, he's not stupid."

Mariah turned the idea over in her mind. "No imagination," she concluded.

They walked quickly along the pavement, back the way they had come.

"It makes good sense to be civil to people," Gwendolyn said. "One may very quickly get a reputation for being unpleasant. And when you need help, nobody wants to know. It doesn't take a lot to work that out. Tolerance. It's like family. You get the ones you like, and the ones you don't like so much. But it makes sense to put a good face on it."

Mariah thought about that for a few moments. How much of her own life would have been better if she had taken that advice in the beginning? But she had done that with her husband, and much good that had been. If only she'd found the courage to stand up to him. How many times had he told her it was her duty to obey him in all matters, but most particularly in intimate ones?

"Mariah?" Gwendolyn said urgently. "Are you all right?" She looked anxious now. "Perhaps I spoke out of turn."

"No!" Mariah said sharply, looking straight into Gwendolyn's eyes. "You are quite right. If you can't escape, you must make the best of it. Stand up for yourself. Or . . ."

"Or what?" Gwendolyn asked. She had no idea what a painful, searching question that was.

"Or leave," Mariah replied, as if it were that simple. "And I am generalizing. We must attend to the particular. Sadie has gone somewhere. It is our duty to her to find out if it was voluntary, and if she is alive and well."

Gwendolyn's face was very sober and a little pale. "Do you think she might be hurt? Lost her memory? Kidnapped?"

That last suggestion was a thought Mariah had not considered. "Why would anyone kidnap her?" she asked. "You mean Barton has been asked for a ransom? Has he any money?" Another thought occurred to her. "Or perhaps he has been told to do something he would not do unless forced. Oh dear." Mariah's mind raced through increasing images of darkness. "Something he would not do unless under extreme pressure? Something even criminal?"

"Yes," Gwendolyn said with a small, tight voice. "Then he would not dare tell anyone. That might be part of the kidnapper's conditions."

"We must order our thoughts," Mariah directed, more to herself than to Gwendolyn. "We are running around like startled chickens. There are only a certain number of reasons a person would leave home suddenly, and without explanation."

Gwendolyn nodded.

"Maybe she ran away on purpose, to escape Barton, or somebody else." Mariah took a sharp breath. "Is there anyone here in St. Helens who is menacing? Is there anything you can think of?"

"Such as . . . what?"

"Something so frightening she had to escape from Barton." Mariah disliked that suggestion. Anyone who is given a second chance at courage must grasp it! "He is not a nice man," she went on. "I would run away before facing him, if I had made a mistake or done something foolish."

Gwendolyn's face was sad now, and serious. "You think that Barton has killed her? Do you? I mean, accidentally, of course! Hit her harder than he meant to?"

Looking at her expression, Mariah dismissed the idea that Gwendolyn was exaggerating or being melodramatic. She meant it, no matter how far-fetched it seemed.

"Do you think he might have disposed of her body because he's afraid her death was in some way his fault?" Mariah asked. "It seems possible, but there are other things, answers less terrible than that. Perhaps she has gone away just to give him a real fright." Another thought flashed in her mind. "Or this is her warning to him that other people will ask, and remember this, if anything should happen to her in the future."

Gwendolyn nodded, her face bleak.

"Or perhaps she has done something wrong, and is afraid she will be punished for it," Mariah suggested again. "Think hard, Gwendolyn. Has anything happened here recently for which she might be blamed?"

Gwendolyn thought for several minutes, until Mariah was about to press her for an answer. Then she spoke, just as Mariah drew breath. "There have been some minor thefts of post. Letters, mainly. A lot of people are talking about it. But really, who wants somebody else's letters and bills? What earthly use are they?"

"To learn private information that someone would pay to keep private? Or to fuel somebody's gossiping for the sake of it?"

Gwendolyn nodded. "I suppose so."

"Can you think of any gossip that could refer to Sadie? Before she was missing?"

"No. Oh dear," said Gwendolyn, her eyes wide with fear. "Do you think she could be dead?"

Mariah took a deep breath. "I think it is unlikely, but of course it is possible. It could be an accident."

"Could it be . . . not an accident?" Gwendolyn's voice was a trifle husky.

"You mean murder? I believe most murders are part of a robbery, or else they are domestic. Or accidents that look like another person's deliberate fault. Maybe Sadie has sent a letter to Barton explaining everything, and it has gone astray."

"If he doesn't know where she is, and he had no part in it, why doesn't he report her disappearance to the police?" Gwendolyn asked.

"Because it's embarrassing," Mariah answered. "They will ask him if he quarreled with her, and he will have to say he did, because I dare say half the village knows what a temper he has. You are sure there is no crime, however petty, that she could be blamed for? Breaking something? Borrowing something and not returning it? Spreading serious gossip that damages someone's reputation?"

Gwendolyn shook her head. "I know of nothing. But still, mustn't we at least see that the neighborhood is searched? All the roads, ditches, copses of trees?"

Mariah shuddered at the thought, but Gwendolyn was right. Being squeamish about the possibilities was a childish excuse not available to a grown woman. "We shall start by listening to the gossip. Most of it will be rubbish, but there may be a kernel of truth somewhere."

"I know just the place to begin," Gwendolyn said. "It's too early now. No one will be there. I'll make a list of what we need at the grocer's, the butcher's, and the greengrocer's. After all, Christmas is nearly here, and we will treat ourselves well." She gave a shy, half-embarrassed smile.

Mariah felt a sudden burst of warmth toward her. "I think that would be an excellent idea," she agreed. "A dish shared is more than twice as good as one taken alone. This is going to be a Christmas remembered for good things as well as all sorts of trouble, which may yet end up well enough."

$\mathcal{T}$hey enjoyed shopping, filling up both the baskets they had brought. Before entering each shop, they agreed between them who was to mention Sadie, Mariah merely saying that she was a friend, in the hope of eliciting some useful response, and Gwendolyn saying that she hadn't seen Sadie for a day or two. But they learned nothing useful.

Then it was time for refreshments at the tea shop on the high street, which was the best place for meeting people in comfort. True to Mariah's expectations, as they walked in the door they were engulfed by the aroma of fresh buns and small cakes, and the sound of women's voices and excited chatter. Mariah recognized a few faces from the past.

At least half of the conversations stopped as Mariah and Gwendolyn came in, carefully closing the door behind them. Mariah could not recall names, except very approximately, and a few details she thought these women would not be pleased to have her remember.

Gwendolyn led the way to the largest empty table, with the full intention that they should be joined as soon as possible.

A waitress came over and asked them what they would like, and Gwendolyn ordered for both of them. They were joined almost immediately by a robust woman who was probably forty years younger than Mariah.

"Dorothy Costigan," she announced. "May I join you?" She sat down without waiting for the answer. She looked straight at Mariah. "You must be Mrs. Ellison. Sadie told us you were coming to stay with her for Christmas. Welcome to St. Helens. How is Sadie? I see she is not with you."

Mariah took the bull by the horns. "I haven't seen Sadie. I arrived yesterday, but Mr. Alsop told me that Sadie was not at home, and he didn't know when to expect her back so, for the sake of propriety, I should look for somewhere else to stay." She made it sound as rude as it had been.

Mrs. Costigan was clearly taken aback, as if she had expected some prevarication. "Oh, my goodness! So, it's true, then?"

"What is true?" Mariah asked, assuming an air of innocence, and hardly able to conceal an *I told you so!* glance toward Gwendolyn.

The woman took a deep breath. "Why, that she has disappeared! It seems nobody knows where she's gone." She leaned forward a fraction. "The big question is, did she go willingly or did someone take her? And what does Barton Alsop know?" She looked from Mariah to Gwendolyn, and then back again.

"You mean that she was kidnapped?" Mariah tried to keep the scorn out of her voice. If she offended this woman, she would learn nothing. The idea now seemed preposterous. But then, the whole situation was preposterous. "For heaven's sake, why? Has Barton Alsop got a great deal more money than anyone supposed? Mrs. Costigan—"

"Please," said the woman, "call me Dorothy. And no, probably not," she said with assurance. "It must be for something else."

"Like what?" Gwendolyn asked, looking totally mystified.

Dorothy's black eyebrows shot up. "I don't know! If I knew anything definite, I would tell the police!"

"But it might be part of the conditions that Mr. Alsop doesn't tell anyone, especially the police," Gwendolyn pointed out.

"What do *you* think happened to her?" Dorothy challenged.

Another woman joined them, inviting herself and taking the fourth chair. She did not introduce herself. Mariah remembered her as Lizzie Putney.

Before the woman could speak, the waitress asked if they would take tea and scones, which they accepted eagerly.

Lizzie Putney answered the question the waitress's

arrival had interrupted. "She went willingly. It would be pretty difficult to snatch someone off the street, you know, without attracting attention. Don't you think so?" This was directed at Mariah, but she did not wait for an answer. "She either went with someone willingly, or perhaps she left the village by herself, to meet someone."

"Just packed a suitcase and left?" Dorothy said with disbelief.

"Why not?" Lizzie demanded. "I've thought of it. And I'll wager most of us have, one time or another. I just wouldn't go alone. Better the devil you know, and all that."

"I've thought of it, too," Dorothy admitted. "Sitting beside the fire, and listening to Mr. Costigan complain about something or another."

Mariah understood perfectly. She, too, had sat in her own chair by the fire, and dreamed of leaving. But the cold, the darkness, no money of her own, public disgrace and private loneliness and fear—all of these had kept her where she was: warm, comfortable, but afraid and desperately lonely. At least that was what she thought Mrs. Costigan was saying.

She turned to Mrs. Putney. "Do you think so?" she asked with the utmost seriousness.

"Something like that," Lizzie replied. "Makes sense. She was always—forgive me for saying so—a little willful. Selfish, and not always honest."

Mariah drew in a sharp breath to defend Sadie and, obliquely, herself. Then, like a dawning light over a familiar landscape, but shown from a different angle, she saw that Lizzie was right.

"Then you consider this honest? Really?" Dorothy said with a sharper tone. "Just to go off somewhere, leaving Barton behind to wonder what has happened to her?"

"Maybe he knows," Lizzie suggested. "He says he doesn't, but that doesn't mean it's true."

"Well, if he does, he's the only one," Dorothy said. "Nobody knows where she is or why she went. She told no one. Not even Mariah here! He told her to go and look for hospitality somewhere else and then he closed the door in poor Mariah's face!"

Mariah was stung. "Poor Mariah" was a deep cut. Nobody wanted to be referred to that way. And she sensed that Dorothy Costigan was beginning to gossip, which was poisonous. Mariah had been on both sides of gossip. As the victim, she had learned that the closer to the truth it was, the deeper the wound. When she had been the carrier of gossip, she had later felt a deep guilt. If she looked within herself, she had to admit that she had gossiped to be the center of attention, the one who knew things that others did not. And to a degree, in her defense, she understood how repeating gossip drew her away from being the subject of other people's wagging tongues.

But now the gossip was aimed at Sadie, even when the situation might be serious, even tragic, and this made Mariah angry.

"She was always a bit scatterbrained," Lizzie was saying. "You don't think she could have just lost her mind altogether, do you? Maybe she's forgotten who she is, or where she lives." She looked from one to another of them, as if someone might actually know the answer.

"No, I don't think that at all!" Mariah snapped.

"Then surely you know something that we don't," Dorothy insisted.

"I know that sitting here talking about Sadie as if she were a lost dog doesn't help anyone," Mariah said. "We must do something useful. Find out who was the last person to see her, or if she said anything that would indicate where she is, and when she intends to come home. If it's a domestic matter, it might be solved without involving the police."

"We can't just ask anybody," Lizzie protested. "We've no right!"

"Will you go and ask Barton Alsop to do it?" Mariah retorted. "It is his place, if we must be official. I doubt you'll get anywhere, except be told to mind your own business." And with that, she stood up, gave Gwendolyn a swift glance, picked up her share of the shopping, left some coins on the table, and went out of the door into the street.

The next door was an estate agent's office, and beyond that a bookshop. She looked in the window, which displayed not only all sorts of publications, including old books, many of them leather bound and with gold lettering, but also large maps, some quite old. She found it interesting to see what shapes people had once imagined the world to be, especially when illustrated with monsters of both land and sea: eagles, lions with wings, monstrous fish named Leviathan.

It was bitterly cold and windy, and the inside looked most inviting. By opening the door, she caught the little bell that hung over it, which chimed pleasantly. An elderly gentleman looked up from the book he had been working on, and put down the blade he was using to trim the replacement leather in its binding.

"Good morning, ma'am," he said courteously. "Are you searching for something in particular, or just looking around?"

Mariah was not sure what she was doing, other than getting out of the icy wind, and leaving the women in the tea shop to gossip. Gwendolyn would tell her if anything useful was said. There was even a hope that with Mariah no longer present, one of them might feel freer to speculate.

"Good morning," she replied. She was still angry, but this man should not have to bear the brunt of her ill temper. "No, I'm not looking for anything special," she replied. "Except a little peace and escape from gossip. I don't want to listen to it, and even more, I don't want to be drawn into it."

He smiled, as if it truly amused him. He had a nice face, weather-beaten, like a man who had spent a lot of time at sea, or in a much hotter climate than England. He also had a full head of silver hair. "Very wise," he said. "A little like shaking hands with an octopus."

For once she was lost for words. The idea was both fascinating and repulsive. A very good description of gossip.

He held out his hand, strong and weathered, like his face. "Oliver Mallard, ma'am. Buyer and seller of things to please the imagination."

She took his hand. "Mariah Ellison. I live in London, but I came here to spend Christmas with an old friend,

Sadie Alsop. Only I find she has gone away, and no one knows where, or why, or for how long. Since she left no message, and her husband appears to know nothing, I am growing concerned. She knew of my arrival because she sent me the timetable, but Mr. Alsop does not know anything about my invitation." She realized she was glaring at this man, as if she expected him to challenge her. She deliberately softened her look. "I'm sorry. I am burdening you with my affairs, when all you did was greet me civilly."

"You look worried," he explained. "And you would be a poor friend if you were not. I know Mrs. Alsop. A spirited and engaging lady."

A curious choice of words, yet they fitted Sadie perfectly. "Have you seen her lately?" Mariah asked.

"About three days ago." He looked completely serious. "She mentioned something about having a friend visit over Christmas. You must be she."

"I am."

"You have known her a long time, yes?"

"Forty years at the very least," she replied. "Maybe fifty. And no, she has never done this before, or anything like it."

"Do you fear that something has happened to her?" he asked gravely.

"I suppose I do," Mariah admitted. "It might not be anything important."

"You don't lie often, do you, Mrs. Ellison?" he said quietly. "You don't do it well."

Mariah drew in breath sharply to give him a curt answer. Then she looked at his face and realized he had her measure, and if she fought him, she would only be making a fool of herself. "I don't know what the truth is," she said quietly.

"What does Mr. Alsop say?"

"Very little. I asked him, but he said she had gone, and he didn't know where, and he wouldn't offer me a bed that night, for decency. For goodness' sake, he's over eighty, and so am I! Not that I wanted to stay there then."

He smiled. "You have other friends in St. Helens?" It was more of a statement than a question.

"Yes. Specifically, Miss Cooper."

"Ah, Gwendolyn. A charming woman."

Mariah felt a momentary stab of envy. She was certain no one had ever described *her* as a charming woman. If she had ever been, which she doubted, the charm had disappeared long ago, consumed by anger and shame. "Yes, she is," she agreed. "And we intend to find out what has happened to Sadie. And, if necessary, help her."

"Brave words, Mrs. Ellison. If I can help you, I would be happy to. I didn't know Mrs. Alsop very well, but I've had a few adventures myself." He said it quietly, and as a matter of fact.

At first, she did not know how to answer him. At last, she said, "We will look ridiculous if she is taking a break or visiting a friend and just forgot the day I was coming." Her voice sounded hollow to her, nearly as absurd as the suggestion.

"What would you prefer?" Oliver asked. "To worry over something that turns out to be merely a lack of consideration, or to have done nothing while Sadie was in desperate trouble and unable to help herself?"

She drew in her breath, then let it out again. He was impossible to lie to, or even make excuses to. "People are coming up with ridiculous, melodramatic theories," she told him. "That Sadie ran off with somebody. That she lost her mind, and her memory, and is wandering around the countryside somewhere. Even that she was kidnapped. No one has suggested that she is lying dead in a ditch, but it is only a matter of time before they do."

"I suppose you have contacted the local hospital?" he asked.

"No, I think only Barton can do that. And if he did, he would be admitting that he doesn't know where she is. I don't think he is ready to do that yet. All I can imagine is that he hopes she will return shortly, and if there is some matter between them, that it will be put aside then. But he is neither a friendly nor approachable man who intends to confide in me."

For a moment, something Mariah perceived as sadness filled Oliver Mallard's expression.

"What does it say that the judgment of the villagers should be more important to him than possibly allowing the police to be unnecessarily troubled?" he said. He looked at her very steadily. "Or is it possible that you believe he is responsible for his wife's leaving . . . ?" He did not complete the thought.

"I'm not sure," Mariah replied miserably. "I'm going to ask the ticket seller at the railway station if he sold her a ticket anywhere." She made an attempt to control her emotion. "If he did not, then either she was kidnapped, or she is still here, but cannot—or chooses not to—contact us." She stopped. She was watching his face, and she wanted to know his reaction before she continued. This search for Sadie was not something she wished to do alone. The darkness was no longer merely gossip that she could dismiss. She herself had been part of forcing it into the open.

"If she has not left by any means we know of," Oliver began, "then we will report her disappearance to Constable Hendershott in the town." There was no hesitation in his tone. "I'm afraid you will have to come with me because you are the one who has a justifiable cause to be looking for her."

"Of course," Mariah agreed. "Shall we go now?" She did not wish to admit her fears. Giving them words was acknowledging their possibilities. "I have nothing more important to do," she finished. "After all, I came here to see Sadie."

Oliver Mallard smiled and rose to his feet. "You do not need to explain yourself to me, Mrs. Ellison."

A wave of anger swept through her. Who was this man that he should even suggest such a thing? He was standing there in front of her, casually dressed in an old seaman's sweater over his shirt, and smiling. At the same time, he looked concerned. For her to throw a fit of selfish temper now would make her ridiculous, a woman imprisoned by her own vanity. She drew in a deep breath. "I was trying to explain myself to myself! I have not done it well, Mr. Mallard. I know that thoughtless actions can make matters worse, not better. I want to do all that is necessary so that nothing ends in disaster that could have been avoided. Thank you, I should be obliged if you came with me."

"I think the police should know. And possibly may even be able to set our minds at ease. Let me get my coat."

It was a brisk walk to the railway station. There was a low wind, but it was ice cold. The thaw of yesterday was now frozen hard on the open roadway. In the fields, drifting patches of overnight snow had not yet melted.

They arrived between trains. The stationmaster, who doubled as the part-time porter, was warming himself by the little stove in his office.

"Stationmaster," Oliver began, holding his hand out.

The other man took it immediately. "Mr. Mallard, sir. How are you?"

"Very well, but a lot troubled. My friend here," he indicated Mariah, "has come to visit her long-time friend, Mrs. Alsop. You know her? Fluffy hair and nice smile."

"Yes, of course I know her. Nice lady. But I haven't seen her since I gave her a copy of the timetable for—" He looked at Mariah. "Would you be Mrs. Ellison, then?"

"Yes, she sent me the timetable, marked with the best train to take," Mariah agreed. "I've come to visit her, but she's not here, and nobody knows where she is."

The stationmaster's face went pale. "Well, she didn't leave on any train from that time to this, and I can swear to it. Unless . . ."

"Unless what?" Mariah demanded.

"Unless she got a ride with somebody," he finished.

"Someone who came to collect her," Oliver added

thoughtfully. "Either someone from here, or someone who came from another village, and took her."

"Like . . . kidnapped?" The stationmaster's voice shook a little.

"Actually, I was thinking she went willingly," Oliver replied. "I hope that it's simply an adventure." He looked at Mariah. "But I agree, we must find out." He gave a tiny smile, just a curve of the lips. "If we interrupt some innocent arrangement, we will apologize and retreat. I, for one, will be happy to find that this is the case."

Mariah could only agree.

"Thank you, Stationmaster," Oliver said.

"Pleasure, sir. You going to find the constable over in Bridgetown?"

"I think we should do that," Oliver said, putting his hand lightly on Mariah's arm.

"Next train's in ten minutes, sir. Only one stop."

Oliver did not ask Mariah. At first, she was inclined to remind him that he did not speak for her, but being honest with herself, she did not mind that he seemed to be taking over. It was the decision she would have made anyway. She would not take any opportunity to bring him down a peg or two until the whole thing was over.

It was not a long trip. At first Mariah intended to sit in silence, but her intentions vanished when Oliver asked her about Sadie, and she found herself recalling adventures and, more often, misadventures of their twenties and thirties. She did not mention her marriage, only the good things. Her marriage seemed distant, like a life that had happened to someone else, and to recall anything of it aloud meant finding words to tell someone, when she preferred to keep bitterness out of her voice. She did not want this man to know the truth at any price at all. It was a wish that surprised her. She pushed away thoughts of her past and dwelled on happy things that she had not thought of for years.

When they finally reached the police station, they went into the small interview room with Constable Hendershott, a young officer, courteous and apparently interested. Oliver sat back and listened while Mariah told her story.

She had rehearsed it in her mind, so the words came quickly, explaining her invitation, and how she'd arrived to find Sadie gone, according to her husband. "He said that she was not at home, and he had no idea where she had gone, or why. She never came home the night before. She has not yet returned, or sent a message. She did not leave by train, according to the stationmaster." She took a deep breath.

The constable frowned. "Why hasn't her husband reported this, Mrs. . . . ?"

"Ellison," she said, "and I don't know. There could be a number of reasons. Embarrassment, for one. But no one in the village seems to know where she is."

"Have you any reason to think that she has come to harm?"

Mariah's mind raced, but came up with nothing substantial.

Oliver leaned forward. "Yes, Constable. Mrs. Alsop invited Mrs. Ellison to stay with her. The village knew about it, and we were expecting her. But no one admits to knowing the whereabouts of Mrs. Alsop. Please take this matter seriously. She may have fallen and be hurt, or even unconscious. We can't ignore it."

"Yes, sir," Constable Hendershott said gravely, nodding his head.

But when they had thanked him and left, Mariah was not sure that the constable was going to do anything, and Oliver Mallard gave her no comfortable assurances to the contrary.

There was a wait of at least half an hour to catch the next train back to St. Helens. Oliver suggested they catch the one after that and have a late lunch at a nearby inn. "They serve the most delicious steak and kidney pudding."

Mariah hesitated in her mind, but not in her answer. "A good idea," she said. "A light suet crust is a delicacy indeed."

"My sentiments exactly."

He took her arm as they crossed the road. She paused for only a moment before she fell into step with him and accepted his assistance. She did not need it; she had crossed every street in her life on her own, especially during her wretched marriage.

They reached the opposite pavement and she gently removed her arm from his hand. On a busy footpath, there was no room to be awkwardly dependent. *Don't make something out of nothing, fool!* she thought to herself.

The restaurant was still serving, only just.

They took their seats in a corner of the dining room. Within a few minutes, they were served. Oliver had not exaggerated. The pudding was rich and savory, beef with kidneys, onions, mushrooms, and carrots, everything cooked perfectly. The pudding on top was remarkably light and also perfectly cooked. Chopped cabbage sat on one side of the plate.

Mariah looked at it and smiled, then gave herself up

to the luxury of a perfect meal and easy conversation about the countryside at this time of year, and the upturn in the book trade at Christmas.

When they finished, they sat for half an hour over coffee. Then they were quite ready to go back to the station and catch the next train to St. Helens.

"I have considered our next move," Oliver said, when they were seated and the train started to pick up speed.

She turned toward him, keen to know what this gentle and considerate man was thinking. "We know now that she did not leave by train," she replied. "Does that mean someone picked her up in a car or gig, or a pony trap of some sort? No one has volunteered that they saw a strange vehicle. Are you suggesting she went at night? It seems so unlikely that she should be out alone after dark. After all, Sadie is my age, or near enough."

"Does that mean she's locked up at sunset?" he asked incredulously, and it sounded like laughter.

"Of course not!" She was confused. "Mr. Mallard, I find many problems with Sadie's disappearance. This weather is too cold for anyone to be outside, let alone lost." Immediately, she wished she had not been so sharp. Was her temper a part of her that she could not change? No, it took more discipline and a nicer personality than she possessed, but it could be done. It must be!

And then she realized that, robbed of anger, she felt

surprisingly gentle, as if she were a frightened child, not a bad-tempered old woman. In fact, was it fear she had tried to hide all those years? The awareness that she was vulnerable, because she was lonely . . . and she cared? No, that was absurd. It would mean she was weak! And that was one truth that must never be admitted.

Oliver then he said gently, "You really are frightened for her, aren't you? I don't think you should give up yet. There's more we can do together, if you are willing." There was a kind yet persistent inquiry in his face.

It would be ridiculous if she did anything but agree. And he was right, it was early afternoon, and there was no reason to give up. Except, she did not know what to do next. And between the tension caused by worry and the pleasure of that delicious meal, she was quite tired.

"It certainly looks as if she did not leave St. Helens," Oliver said thoughtfully.

Mariah realized its full import as he said it, and she saw the concern deepen in his face.

"I'm afraid this is so," she said quietly. It was not the conclusion she wanted to reach.

"How well do you know her?"

He did not need to emphasize the importance of the question: the gravity in his face was more meaningful than his choice of words. She had the strong impression that he had dealt with grave matters before, perhaps often. Maybe there was no crisis that would make him panic, or lose that ability to face, rather than evade, trouble. He deserved a completely honest answer.

"I used to know her quite well, when we were many years younger. At least, I thought I did. But I am reconsidering, and I realize that perhaps I didn't." She hesitated. How deep an answer did he want? How deep an answer could she give?

He drew breath to speak, and then apparently decided to remain quiet.

"I have changed in the last few years," she went on. "And I saw myself in the past quite differently. It was not always a pleasant experience." Should she be telling him this? It was not what he had asked. And yet the more she thought about it, the more it really was. "If Sadie has changed as much as I have, then I may not know her at all."

He waited in silence, his expression urging her on.

"What I mean is, she may not be the person I believed her to be. Perhaps my judgment was kinder than deserved because I wished it to be." She was thinking of some of the unkind things she and Sadie had done in the past. She had thought them justified. Now, they looked mean in spirit. "People can change in a year or two, never mind a couple of decades."

"Do you think she might have gone somewhere deliberately, just to create a stir, and the type of concern she has caused?" He looked at her steadily.

If she told him less than the truth, she had the sudden conviction that she would be betraying the new self she so badly wanted to become. "Yes," she admitted. "That is what I fear."

"So, we should consider this as possibly an intentional disappearance? Not necessarily a disaster?"

"I think so, but I—"

"—would not say so to others," he finished for her. "We must not stop looking for her or examining all possibilities."

"Exactly," she agreed. "And we should not panic! I fear that she might have gone somewhere miles away, with somebody, possibly a man she knows."

"Would she do that?" The expression on his face gave no indication as to his feelings about a woman who would run off and leave everyone, including her husband, in ignorance and fear. Was Sadie so selfish? Or was she so desperate, and no one had noticed?

"How much do we really know about each other?" Mariah said. "We say, 'How are you?' and then reply,

'Fine, very well, thank you.' And we don't mean it, neither the question nor the answer. It's like asking, 'How do you do?' when nobody really wants to know."

She remembered saying just that, when the last thing she wanted to know was how someone was. When she was asked, she was tempted to answer that she was growing old, full of aches that sometimes frightened her, bored with doing the same pointless things day after day, and so lonely she could weep. But, of course, she did not say that.

"Perhaps Gwendolyn could give us some better insight, if you asked her?" Oliver suggested. This was not a matter of politeness, something harmless and meaningless to say. "But before that, I think we should go and speak with Barton Alsop. Either he already knows where Sadie is—and we push to persuade him to tell us. Or if he does not know, he must join us in searching for her. Whatever has happened, the mystery must be solved. Do you agree?"

"Yes, I do. We can do nothing further without speaking to him." She nearly added "thank you," but what he was suggesting was only the right thing to do. It had nothing to do with Mariah or her anxiety. "I can justify my concern to Barton Alsop. I could go back to London, but I must stay here in case Sadie returns. I want to know if Sadie—no, I *need* to know—why she invited me and then made no provision for me. This is something she would not willingly do, of that much I am certain. Barton won't shut the door in my face again, as he would if I were alone."

Oliver nodded his agreement, and then leaned back in his seat and watched the countryside with the same pleasure she did. The issue was settled, for now.

$\mathcal{M}$ariah was right. In the late afternoon, when she stood beside Oliver Mallard on Sadie's front step, Barton Alsop opened the door, looked at Oliver with distaste, but did not close the door against them. At the same time, Mariah could see that Barton was not brave enough to defy him. He looked troubled and there were deep shadows under his eyes, but it was evident that he had made the effort to shave. Mariah felt a sudden lurch of pity for him.

"Good afternoon. It's Mallard, isn't it? From the bookshop?" Barton asked.

"Yes, and Mrs. Ellison, whom I believe you have known for many years," Oliver replied.

Barton stood in the middle of the doorway, blocking

their view of the hall, and clearly not willing to move. "Yes," he agreed. "We have known each other casually, and at some distance, for a very long time. But it is absurd that she should now claim to know me, just because she sees my wife for a few days, every so many years. That is both knowing, and merely being acquainted and not knowing at all. I'm sorry she has been inconvenienced." He spoke to Oliver, exactly as if Mariah were not there at all.

Mariah glanced at Oliver, and her retort died on her lips. She must keep her temper. Rudeness was an escape. She knew that now. She left it to Oliver to answer.

"It is not inconvenience that concerns Mrs. Ellison," Oliver replied. "It is her need to know whether Sadie has come to some harm. A small accident, perhaps, but one that has prevented her from sending any message."

"Such as what, for heaven's sake?" Barton's eyebrows rose in disbelief, but there was both pain and hope in his face, as if that was an answer he would have loved to accept.

Oliver took a deep breath. Mariah, watching his face, realized that he was profoundly angry. It was not thwarted interest or offense at rudeness, it was a fear of something much darker. The light had waned a little and the lamps were on in houses, where colored paper chains hung across curtains and bright Christmas wreaths adorned every door, incongruous with the mood here.

"Perhaps she has no way to send a message to you," Oliver suggested. "Or perhaps the cause is more serious, like illness. Or worse." He was looking at Barton's face, and must now see what Mariah saw: fear.

Oliver's expression was suddenly more intense. "I don't suppose you have been asked for money for her safe return?" He stopped.

Alsop's face was suddenly robbed of all life. He stared at Oliver as if he were the only being on earth. Mariah had ceased to exist, as had the colored lights of the other houses, and the chill wind still blowing down the road, rustling the last few dried leaves. "No." The word was barely audible.

"Because if you have," Oliver went on, "and you were threatened if you went to the police, you will need their help. Were you asked for money? Or to do something in return for your wife's freedom?"

Mariah could see that Oliver was not going to leave until he was answered, and she could also see that Alsop realized that as well.

Alsop backed away from the door, allowing Mariah to step inside, out of the icy air, with Oliver Mallard on her heels.

Alsop led the way, not to the sitting room but to the kitchen, where there were several cups on the table. He left Oliver and Mariah to sit or stand, as he sank into the nearest chair. "No one has asked for anything," he said, his voice drained of any emotion. "Not a word. I haven't any money, beyond our regular needs, but I never thought of that." He stared at Oliver. "Why don't they ask? What are they waiting for?"

Oliver sat down in the chair opposite Alsop and Mariah took the one beside it. "What do you think, Mr. Alsop? This will be the third night she has been gone. Where did you think she was? And why? Even more, why no word?"

"We quarreled about some stupid thing. I can't remember what, just the usual. Not over any particular issue."

You quarreled for the sake of it, Mariah thought. She could remember doing that often, lashing out because she was hurt and she wanted to hurt back.

"Are you sure?" Oliver pressed.

"Quarrels don't need a reason," Mariah said. She could remember this, even through all the words she wanted to forget. Cruel words had come easily to her, and it was one thing she and Sadie had in common. She realized that now. Otherwise, they were so different.

It was Gwendolyn who could brush aside a cruel remark and make it sound trivial, even foolish. Mariah was never able to do that. She pushed from her mind scenes from her own marriage. It damaged her to think of them, and no one else knew or cared. "Did you hit her?" she demanded, looking intently at Barton.

"How dare you suggest that!" Barton began, but his flushed face was full of guilt.

Mariah did not look at Oliver. "So, she went in anger," she concluded.

"For God's sake! I didn't hit her hard. I merely slapped her!" This time it was shame filling his face.

Mariah felt momentarily better. Now there was some reason for Sadie going off and forgetting her friend's arrival.

Oliver looked from one to the other of them, his expression unreadable. "You're saying she left in a temper?"

Alsop nodded. "Yes. I'm afraid she has a very hot temper. But I saw no reason to tell Mariah that," he said, glancing at Mariah, giving her a hard look, and then back to Oliver. "She—Mariah, that is—wouldn't understand, since she has the filthiest temper I have ever seen. And considering Sadie's behavior, that is saying a great deal."

Mariah was overcome with emotion, although she was not sure if she was feeling indignation or shame. Perhaps both. She said nothing, but it took great control to keep her expression neutral, passive.

"But it was you who lost your temper, yes?" Oliver asked quite gently. "Do you really think she intended to be gone for days?"

"No, of course not!" Barton's anger was gone, replaced by undisguised anxiety. "I didn't say anything to begin with because I knew she was just exercising her temper. No self-control." He glanced at Mariah, and then back again at Oliver. "Thank you for your concern, but it is not necessary. Sadie's throwing a tantrum, a melodramatic one, even for her."

Mariah struggled with accepting his words. They were not enough. "So, she is too embarrassed to come home?" She took a deep breath. "You need to go and tell her that you want her back, and you will make peace. Or . . ." She took another breath. She knew Oliver was watching her. "Don't you want her back?"

"This is where she belongs," Alsop said, desperation now in his voice. "I don't know what's the matter with her. She is—" This time, when he stopped, it was clearly because he did not know how to continue.

Oliver must have heard what Mariah did, because

his expression softened. "If you know where she is, you can go and fetch her."

"She can come home anytime she wants—" Alsop began.

"She may not know that," said Oliver, cutting him off.

"If you know where she is, then go and get her!" Mariah snapped.

Alsop looked at the floor, then up again at Mariah. His face was ashen. "I tried that, but she wasn't there. I swear! She was at the cottage on Briar Lane, the one standing empty, that's for sale. But she's taken her things, and there's no way to tell where she went from there."

"Taken them?" said Mariah. "As if she didn't mean to come back?"

"Yes." It was just the one, bleak word.

"I know the cottage you mean," Oliver said. "A good place to hide. Although it's for sale, no one is likely to come to look at it the week before Christmas. You are sure she's been there?"

"Yes," Alsop answered with certainty. He avoided looking at either Oliver or Mariah. He was clearly embarrassed. "I went there the first evening, after dark, and I saw her in the lighted window. She looked relaxed, even . . . satisfied."

Mariah could imagine it very easily. Unless they were looking at the cottage specifically, no one was likely to notice the light. The front garden was larger than usual, and full of bushes and trees. She had seen the cottage ages ago and had liked the look of it. If she remembered correctly, she had even daydreamed of owning such a place. Ridiculous, of course.

"But you're quite sure she's not there now?" Oliver pressed.

"No. I went back last night and there were no lights, even though it was dark outside. I peered in through the windows but it was completely dark." He looked at both of them, all self-confidence gone. "I don't know what to do."

"We'll think very carefully," Oliver answered him. Then he rose to his feet. "Meanwhile, if you think of anything else, Mr. Alsop, let us know."

Mariah stood also, as did Alsop.

"Thank you," Alsop said quietly. "It is good of you to speak of it to me and not behind my back." He glanced at Mariah, including her in the remark.

"Gossip is the coward's way," she said, then instantly wondered if she had been too forthright. She glanced at Oliver, who did not try to hide his amusement.

Alsop lit the outside lantern so they could see their way clearly on the steps down to the front path.

Mariah reached the lowest step, where she had to tread carefully. She looked down and saw, in the light from the hall and the lantern, the amber-colored wood and a dark stain. She stopped abruptly, almost losing her balance.

Oliver looked down also. The stain was liquid, dark red. Like blood.

Suddenly, Mariah felt a cold chill forming deep inside herself.

Oliver gripped her arm. "Step around it," he said quietly, his mouth close to her ear. "Keep walking." And to give urgency to his words, he pulled her forward, then held her firmly as they went down the path, and heard Alsop close the door.

Her heart was hammering. She walked out onto the footpath, still clinging to his arm.

He left her there and returned to the steps. After kneeling for a closer look, he peered at the edge of the flowerbed. He straightened and moved quickly to where Mariah was waiting. "A dead mouse."

"Are you sure?"

"Quite sure," he said. "Harmless, and undoubtedly gone by morning."

"You think Barton Alsop will clean it up?" she asked, a tinge of disbelief in her voice.

"This is the countryside. Small animals get killed. And yes, before you say so, people do, too. I know that. Now we must go; it's too cold to linger."

"*I*'m sorry," Mariah said to Gwendolyn, when at last she reached what was her temporary home. Oliver had said good night to her, offered a courteous good-night to Gwendolyn, and then walked away from them, following the street as it disappeared into the gathering darkness.

"Are you all right?" Gwendolyn demanded. "Did you learn anything? I didn't. At least nothing that I didn't know, or could deduce. You look cold. Are you hungry?"

Mariah hesitated only a moment. "I had a wonderful lunch, but yes, I'm hungry now. I'm sorry to be so long."

Gwendolyn smiled. "You left here this morning, so it must feel like a long time. It's important that you enjoy yourself, but that's no longer the point, is it? Did you learn anything?"

Mariah followed Gwendolyn through to the kitchen. They sat at the scrubbed wooden table, where they savored cups of tea and ginger biscuits. She told Gwendolyn as much as she now knew, and something of what she surmised, or even feared. She mentioned the blood on Sadie's front step.

"What are you going to do?" Gwendolyn asked, her eyes searching Mariah's face anxiously. "Do you know whose blood?"

"It was a mouse!" Mariah said, relief in her voice.

"Thank God," Gwendolyn said quietly. "Mariah, we must find her. This isn't some imaginary courtroom drama, this is real. Maybe it wasn't her blood this time, but—" She paused. "You're a practical person." She gave a tight little smile. "We all evade some truths, if we can, but you're pretty good at not doing that, or letting other people do it either." She took a deep breath and did not look away from Mariah's eyes. "We need the truth, whether we choose to see it or not. We'll have to live with it, whatever happens."

Mariah sat totally still. She had always seen Gwendolyn as the quiet younger sister, the girl in Annabel's shadow. The one who had not married, who had been obliged to take a job as some kind of worker with books and papers, suitable for a single woman. Social acceptance depended on her making the best of it, and not complaining. Complaints, however justified, were extremely boring to other people.

Mariah paused to consider these thoughts, and then realized how superficial they were.

It was at that moment that her mind was made up. "Tomorrow, as early as possible, I'll go to that empty house and see if Sadie is there. Perhaps Barton missed something. She's somewhere! And we have not found any evidence of her having left the village."

"You can't go alone," Gwendolyn protested, but with a sudden vitality that made her eyes bright, and caused her to sit straighter on the kitchen chair. "I'll go with you. What about Oliver? Should we tell him where we're going, so that if we don't come back, he can come and look for us? Or report it to the police?"

Mariah's mind whirled. Yes, it would be foolish to go alone. She realized she had imagined he would come with her, which was ridiculous. He had already done more than his duty, both to help Mariah and, more important, to try to find Sadie. She could not ask him to give up more of his time. No matter how generous he was, he would think her a nosy, selfish old woman who sought more attention than she was entitled to. Worse than that, he might realize she was at ease with him, and found him intelligent and most comfortable. That was because she never needed to wonder if he understood, and found it interesting that he knew so many things she did not. She wondered if he represented most men, and that those of her late husband's temperament were the exception and not the rule.

But to deny Gwendolyn would be inconceivable. And she was waiting for an answer. The light was dying out of her eyes as Mariah hesitated. "Are you sure you want to come?" she asked, as if she had been weighing it in her mind. "It could be unpleasant."

"All the more reason you should not go alone," Gwendolyn answered.

"You and I," Mariah said. "We can tell Oliver what we find."

Gwendolyn nodded. "But we still should plan just—"

"Plan?"

"Yes! What are we going to say to her?" Gwendolyn asked. "Before we tell her the trouble she has caused us, and the anxiety, we had better ask why she has done such a seemingly selfish and rather childish thing. She has caused a great deal of worry, most of all to Barton." The expression in her eyes was both sad and angry. "Which, of course, was probably her intention."

"That's a little extreme," Mariah replied.

Gwendolyn gave her tight little smile again, but not without humor. "Oh, really? Sadie? Surely not—"

"All right," Mariah said ruefully. "Of course, if she did this on purpose, it was to gain attention. But I'm trying hard to think well of her, and allow for other answers." She felt self-conscious as she said this, but it was true. She herself had regretted too much. She must lessen the load of all that old guilt, not add to it.

"Let's find her first," Gwendolyn said soberly. "She had ... well, if she is in that cottage, she—" She stopped, as if unable to form the words.

"She may be dead," Mariah said for her.

Gwendolyn paled, but her eyes looking at Mariah did not waver. "Which would explain why she has said nothing, sent no message—why she wasn't at home for you."

Mariah's mind raced, one idea melting into another. She could not deny the possibility that Sadie was indeed dead. It was a cold, miserable, violent thought.

"Yes, you are right," she said with a nod. "We need to know what has happened, but we must be careful. I suggest we go as early as we can be ready."

They said their good-nights and Mariah walked slowly to her room, fatigue wrapping itself around her. She intended to read a bit, but once in the warmth of the bed, she was unable to stay awake.

*I*n the morning, feeling rested and refreshed, Mariah entered the kitchen and found Gwendolyn laying out the utensils for breakfast.

They ate in silence, lost in their thoughts, both focused on the hope of finding Sadie alive.

With breakfast consumed, Gwendolyn rose to her feet, carried the dishes to the sink, then went to fetch her coat, scarf, hat, and gloves, with Mariah following close behind.

It was a pleasant walk, but not a day for standing around talking to people. They went directly to the cottage. It was a little over half a mile, but the roads were icy and one could slip if not paying attention. All the houses they passed were decorated in one way or another for Christmas. The more conservative homes had merely a colored wreath on the door. Gwendolyn pointed out that those with children had something more imaginative. Mariah particularly enjoyed how one family had tied red ribbons to the well-pruned rosebushes. It was as if, in place of flowers, they had grown satin bows.

The cottage they were seeking was easy to recognize, with its large, overgrown garden, apparently neglected for some time, even before its owners had moved out. From a distance, they could see several trees, mostly with bare branches, their type determined only by the patterns of the growth, or the markings on the trunks. The birches were easy to recognize, due to their slender, white-patterned trunks, as were, of course, the willows.

Now that they were there, Mariah felt less confident about what to do, but she did not want Gwendolyn to see her misgivings. As much as she wished she had a better idea, one that did not necessitate going into a deserted house, she felt they had no choice. What were they going to do if they knocked and no one came to the door? The answer came to her mind, as if it had been waiting to pounce. They would break in!

She gave Gwendolyn a quick glance as they reached the front door. Gwendolyn took a quick, deep breath, reached for the bell rope, and pulled it. They could hear the bell ringing somewhere far inside the house. They waited a full minute, then another. Gwendolyn gave the bell a harder pull. Again, there was no answer.

"If we are going to break in, we had better not do it at the front, where one can be seen from the street," Mariah said determinedly. "Are you—"

"Yes," Gwendolyn answered before she could finish the sentence. "If Sadie is there, she can't, or won't, answer the door." She stopped, took a deep breath to continue, then seemed to change her mind.

Mariah was glad that Gwendolyn had not continued.

91

Everything she could think to say would only make the situation worse. There were many alternatives possible: Sadie was there and had no wish to be found, or she had suffered injury or illness and could not answer. She could have been there and then left. Mariah used to think that making other people think her a fool was the worst thing that could happen to her. She had feared people who feigned horror, and the sniggers of laughter behind her that it seemed would never cease. Now she did not care. It was what she thought of herself that she had to live with. There was one last possibility, which she preferred not to consider too closely: Sadie was inside, and she was dead.

"Come." She beckoned Gwendolyn, and they walked carefully around the side of the house, and followed the path to the kitchen door. Along the way, both of them looked to see if there were any windows open, or a door left unlocked, or any other means of getting inside.

They stood at the back door. The upper part was glass. Ridiculous. Anyone could break it and get in. Mariah was sure that if this were her house, she would replace that door with a proper wooden one. But then, she lived in London. Out here, there probably hadn't been a crime in years.

Gwendolyn tried the handle. "It's locked," she said quietly. "But we could break the glass, couldn't we?"

Mariah hesitated.

"If she's in there, hurt, it would be awful if we just walked away and left her," Gwendolyn said in a hushed voice, as if there were neighbors nearby who could hear her.

Mariah thought about it. What on earth would her granddaughter's husband, the policeman, think of her? He would be appalled! No, he wouldn't—he'd be surprised. And in spite of his official disapproval, he would most probably laugh! But more important, he would understand.

"We need to find where we can reach the lock and all the bolts, and then undo them," she said. "Not much point breaking the glass if we still can't get in. Is there a window? Check for one over the sink."

Gwendolyn moved a little further from the door and returned at once. "Yes, and it's large. One of us could climb in. I'll do it, and then I'll go to the door and let you in."

Mariah was about to protest when she realized that Gwendolyn was almost five inches taller than she was, and her legs were correspondingly longer. And she was younger! Any protest died on her lips. They needed common sense and efficiency, not vanity. "Right," she agreed.

They moved to a side window. It was not the largest downstairs, but seemed the most accessible.

"This one is best," Gwendolyn pointed out. "I know I can get through it, and there seems to be a bench of some sort on the other side."

Mariah was about to ask what use this was, when she realized that at least there would be something for Gwendolyn to land on. If they were caught, what on earth were they going to say? But that was another matter, to be faced only when necessary.

Mariah was reminded again how much younger Gwendolyn was when she watched her climb onto a dustbin, careful not to overturn it, and make a single blow against the window with a stone. Before climbing through, she carefully broke all the dagger edges of remaining glass capable of cutting badly, even fatally. She did this without caution: there was no use pretending the window had been broken by accident. Mariah pointed out one large shard in the corner and Gwendolyn immediately dealt with it.

Mariah's respect for Gwendolyn was growing with every minute. It flickered through her mind to wonder if Annabel had any idea how much more there was to Gwendolyn than met the eye. Or did John Spears know? At one time, he would have married either sister. Had he made the right choice? Gwendolyn was infinitely kinder than Annabel and made a charming companion. Still, it was too late now.

Mariah was pulled away from her thoughts when she realized that Gwendolyn was inside. She heard her footsteps on the wooden floor, then the rasp of the bolts being drawn back on the door. She stepped inside the moment it was open.

The house was cold, even with the door shut, but not as bad as Mariah had expected. She looked around the scullery. There were two big sinks, both empty. One of them was clean, the other held a fine layer of dust. She went over to the big iron cooker, with its hot plates on top and the stove beneath. Slowly, as if it might burn her, she touched the fire door, where it would be regularly stoked to keep everything hot. It was warm! Only just, but warm nevertheless. Mariah touched the other metal parts, further from the fire. They were definitely cold. She swung round to face Gwendolyn, and Mariah could see by her companion's expression that she understood.

"Warm?" Gwendolyn asked.

Mariah nodded. "Someone has been here, maybe as recently as yesterday." She pointed out crumbs on the table, not yet dried to brittleness, and a jug of milk. She picked it up and sniffed. "Still fresh," she said in answer to Gwendolyn's look.

"Then where is she now?" Gwendolyn asked. She dropped her voice until it was barely more than a whisper. "Do you think she's still here? Somewhere?" She looked up at the ceiling, as if half expecting to hear footsteps. "Do you suppose she's upstairs?"

"Then why did she let the fire die?" Mariah looked round at the coal scuttle by the stove. It was still half full. "It's a lot easier to keep a fire going than it is to let it go out."

"Maybe she's gone, then," Gwendolyn said, again glancing upward. "She hasn't come down to see who broke the glass, and if she's here she must have heard it."

Mariah gave the only answer that came to mind. "Either she can't, or she is afraid to. That is, if she *is* still here." She took another deep breath. "We must go upstairs and look in case she is ill or hurt." Mariah knew she needed to go quickly, before she had time to think it through, with the possibility of ridicule, outrage, or even the danger that might result.

She picked up the poker from the bucket beside the stove and walked over to the door leading into the hallway. The soft sounds of Gwendolyn's footsteps behind her were comforting.

There was no one in the sitting room, made light by its bay windows. It was well furnished, and Mariah could see that it could be charming, even beautiful. When she had first arrived, it had been only the garden whose possibilities tantalized her, but now the proportions and the simplicity of the sitting room charmed her as well. The windows had only one curtain remaining. The garden outside was desolate in the cold, pale light. The advent of spring would make it completely different. She was certain that one would find new life in it as the sun warmed it.

She turned her attention to the room. Before she could speak, Gwendolyn announced, "Mariah, there's nothing to show anyone's been in here. Even the fireplace is clean."

"I see that," Mariah replied quietly. "Let's try the other rooms."

They went up the strong wooden staircase to the top floor and almost immediately into the main bedroom. It was light, a white-windowed space looking out over the back garden. Much like the garden in front, it was untidy and overgrown. Even from this distance, Mariah could see that the soil was rich.

She turned away from its possibilities and looked at the big bed. It was rumpled, not so much untidy as . . . she wasn't sure. There was the outline of a small body, but not a child, rather a small adult. She walked over to it and moved the covers very slightly. She found several hairs, almost three inches long. They were light gold in color, but white at the root. An old woman's hair.

Mariah and Gwendolyn exchanged a glance.

"Definitely Sadie's," concluded Gwendolyn. "But why did she come here? If it was just to get away from Barton because of their argument, why did she leave and where has she gone now?"

"I don't understand any of it." Mariah stared at Gwendolyn while searching her mind for an answer, one that made sense.

Before leaving, they checked the bathroom. What they immediately saw caused them to stop in their tracks, eyes wide in horror. On the rim of the sink was a dark red smudge.

They stepped closer. Mariah was holding her breath, as was Gwendolyn.

"Don't touch it," instructed Mariah quickly. "The police need to see it just as it is."

"Can it be anything but blood?" asked Gwendolyn.

"I don't know anything else that looks quite like that," said Mariah, gulping nervously. "Do you?"

Gwendolyn's silence, the grim set of her mouth, was the answer.

They bent forward, peering at the blood closely.

"Do you see this?" Gwendolyn asked, pointing to several hairs embedded in the ooze.

The hairs were long, the same blond with white roots.

"Sadie's," confirmed Gwendolyn.

Mariah released a deep breath. "We don't know for sure," she said with little hope in her voice. "And if it is, did she fall, or was she attacked?"

They stood in silence for a long moment, and then Mariah spoke. "This changes everything." Her voice was not quite as steady as she would have liked it to be. "Sadie is not here, so either she escaped—in which case, why has no one seen her?—or she has been injured and taken to a different place, where she is being held."

"But, why?" Gwendolyn asked. "Has someone . . . what? I don't know! If they kidnapped her, do you suppose they've threatened Barton that if he told anyone, they would . . ."

She stopped short of saying the word, but Mariah heard it in her own mind as clearly as if she had said it herself. "No," she said decisively. "She's no use to them dead."

"But if Barton didn't pay a ransom—or whatever it is they want—what else could they do except let her go? Maybe they can't do that because she knows who they are . . ." Gwendolyn's voice trailed off again, as if she were afraid to put her thoughts into words. There was no need to speak them; the fear was evident in her face.

After a long moment, Mariah said, "There is something important about this, something that we haven't learned, but we must. If"—she swallowed hard—"if Sadie's life is in danger, and judging by the blood, we must assume that it is . . ."

"Maybe she's gone back home, her head wounded by a fall, and we just don't know yet?" Gwendolyn suggested with a lift of hope in her voice. And then she paused, as if saying any more might stop it from being true.

Mariah wanted to be gentle. She liked Gwendolyn, and that was apart from being grateful to her for making Mariah welcome in her house. But she was frightened that this situation might indicate some kind of a tragedy. "We must tell what we have found," she told her. "But only what we have to," she added hastily. "I expect everyone in the village is aware that Sadie has disappeared. Anything we say will be known in a matter of hours. Unless she's gone home and we just don't know it yet, Sadie is still in danger. That is, if you think she's not part of it. Could she be?"

"Part of it?" Confusion clouded Gwendolyn's face.

"Her disappearance," Mariah clarified. "Could she have planned it all, to bring attention to herself? It started as a row with Barton and now she's exacting some extreme revenge."

Gwendolyn took a long moment before responding. "I

don't understand this at all. Sadie is a bit selfish, and she can be cruel. But that's just how she is, how she has always been."

Mariah nodded. "But perhaps we're wrong about what has happened." Before Gwendolyn could respond, she continued, "The only thing that matters now is that we find her and then see what the truth is. I can imagine someone disappearing to get attention, but intentionally injuring herself? Drawing blood? I can't believe she would take it that far." She paused for a moment, trying to put reason to her thoughts. "I think we should ask for Oliver Mallard's help again," she decided. Even to her ears, her voice betrayed her fear. "He has shown sincere concern."

"Are you sure he's the person to go to?" Gwendolyn asked.

"Certainly," Mariah replied, and so quickly that it forced her into a position where it would be impossible, humiliating even, not to ask him.

*T*here was no time to waste. Mariah went to the bookshop in the high street straightaway, before she could change her mind, or think of the reasons why it would be embarrassing, and not at all the way a lady would behave. She pushed all that from her mind and concentrated on keeping her balance on the icy pavement, while at the same time not attracting the attention of other people she knew, even if only slightly, should they be walking nearby.

Someone stopped to speak to her, and she looked straight ahead, pretending she had not seen them. She was old enough to get away with that, which she considered unfortunate! Were it any other time, she would have denied even the possibility of being deaf or short-sighted.

She reached the bookshop and realized there might be other customers. Was this really so important that it gave her the right to interrupt? Yes, it was. And it was also best kept secret, or at least extremely discreet. This was a shop, a place of commerce, not a private home. It would be ridiculous to knock! She opened the door and walked in. The shop's bell rang quite softly, but it sounded sharp and loud to her.

There was nobody there. But there had to be: the door was unlocked.

"Mr. Mallard!" she called out loudly. It sounded demanding, not at all pleasant to her ears, but it was impossible to take back. But wasn't that true of so many things she had said through the years? Bitter things, cruel and unkind, complaining, and self-centered.

Suddenly, Oliver Mallard was there before her, as if materializing out of the air. She supposed he had been behind one of the bookshelves.

"Good morning, Mariah," he greeted politely, and then he looked at her curiously. "Is something wrong? You look distressed."

She was thrown off her purpose for being there. When was the last time a man had called her by her first name? Should she correct him? Or perhaps simply accept that this indicated he considered her a friend. She pushed aside the subject entirely and thought about the cottage and the blood. "I'm sorry to intrude, and to shout," she added, feeling flustered. "But I— we—have made a discovery, and would like your advice." She closed her eyes. This was someone whose good opinion mattered to her, and she was barging in as if she had some extraordinary right to behave like this.

"I will close the shop so we are not disturbed," Oliver said, sensing the seriousness of the matter. "Very few people call here without an appointment."

He walked over to the door, turned round the "Open" sign so that it read "Closed," and then returned. He gestured to the seat on the other side of the table.

After they were both seated, he spoke first, with a sense of urgency. "What has happened?"

His tone struck her as practical and businesslike. She began matter-of-factly, and without having to reach for words. "Gwendolyn and I went to look at the cottage where Barton Alsop told us Sadie had gone, near the end of Briar Lane."

His eyes were bright with interest, but he did not interrupt her. He simply nodded and waited for her to continue.

She took a deep breath. There was no good purpose to be served by shading the truth. "I'm afraid we broke a window, and climbed in. That is, Gwendolyn climbed in. And then she went to the back door and opened it for me."

"Neither of you was hurt?" he quickly asked.

"No. But someone will have to replace the window, or at least nail a board over it. We made certain to break a window at the back, one that was invisible from the street."

"I will attend to it," Oliver offered instantly. "But that is not the reason you're here. Tell me, what did you find?" He was leaning forward a fraction, his face alive with interest.

"We found evidence that someone has been there recently," she replied. "The iron stove in the kitchen was still warm." She drew in a sharp breath. She had been so certain that she knew what she was going to tell him, but now it did not sound like anything positive. And she was still feeling the same fear, but without its clarity.

He was waiting, not interrupting nor prompting her.

"Someone had been in the bedroom at the back, and I'm assuming it was Sadie. I suppose that was so she could move about freely, without the possibility of being seen from the road. In any case, someone had slept in the bed, and then it seems that they left in a hurry. There was still an indentation on the mattress." The memory made her tremble. "And it was made by a small person, a bit taller than I am, but not very heavy." She took a deep breath to steady herself. "Whoever it was has fair hair, like Sadie's. And before you say that I haven't seen Sadie in years, it was Gwendolyn who said it was almost certainly her hair."

Oliver continued to sit without moving, his lips tight together. It was several moments before he spoke. "Did you find anything to indicate that she had been tied up or restrained in any way?"

Mariah opened her mouth to speak, and then stopped suddenly. What was heavy on her mind sat like a large rock. "Blood."

He leaned back, almost as if having been struck.

"On the bathroom sink."

"Dear God," he said gravely, just above a whisper.

"I think she was there quite willingly at first, as Mr. Alsop said. Hiding, not kidnapped."

He moved his head a fraction, as if listening even more intently.

"Just to draw attention," she went on, assuming that was the unasked question. "But then someone came. I believe that's when Sadie was attacked and forced to leave unwillingly." She nearly apologized for making these assumptions, but Oliver was clearly listening and agreeing.

His eyes, as they met hers, were perfectly steady.

She felt less self-conscious, and in a way emboldened to continue. "There were several signs of her having been there without fear. The breadcrumbs on the table were fresh. And the milk was still sweet. Someone must have brought her those things. She didn't creep out and get them herself." Was she grasping for answers, stretching her mind to re-create something out of nothing real? "The blood on the sink was still damp."

"There's no way of knowing that it's Sadie's blood," he pointed out.

"There were hairs in the blood that looked like the

ones we found on the pillow. Gwendolyn is certain it belongs to Sadie. I think she was there until shortly before we arrived." She paused briefly, waiting to see if Oliver believed her. His eyes were narrowed and he was nodding slowly. "Sadie is in grave danger." She drew in her breath, waiting for his arguments. None came.

Mariah sat back and waited. She was sure it was the right choice, telling him. While it was true that she had known him only since the previous day, which was hardly enough to judge him, she felt comfortable with him.

"Mariah, you're saying that she went there willingly, but did not leave of her own volition." He paused for a moment, mulling this over in his mind. "I can see your point."

She searched his face. He seemed as concerned, even as frightened, as she was, and she felt relief that he was not going to try to contradict her. "Yes, I do believe she may have gone to the house willingly, even with someone's help, someone who was bringing her food. Did that person turn on her? Or did someone search for her, attack her, and then take her away by force? All of that fits what we saw."

Oliver frowned. "What do you think they want to achieve?"

She analyzed his face. He was totally serious, not doubting or mocking her. Speaking to her as an equal. And there was sharp concentration in his wind-burned face, in those strong, gentle features and steady eyes. Normally, she would have been defensive, but she was sure she respected him, and was hoping to earn his respect in return. And respect, she knew, can only be earned. To pretend to respect when you don't could be a dangerous lie, an insult, one creating an unbridgeable gulf between people. "I don't know," she confessed quietly. "As I've told you, I've known Sadie for years, decades, since we were young. But we've changed, perhaps more than I realized. I see some of myself in her, or I think I do, and I'm not sure I like it. Being similar is only relevant because I think I understand her, how she thinks. To begin with, I wonder if she's done this for attention. She knows that we would celebrate Christmas, because we have all prepared for it, but everybody's mind would be on Sadie. *Where is she? Why would she go? Who took her? Is she alive now, or is she dead?* I can't help thinking that the Sadie I knew would reappear at just the right time and make her grand entrance."

A shadow of comprehension crossed Oliver's face. "Arriving at the church, in the middle of the Watch Night service?"

She refused to smile at the vision it conjured in her mind.

"If we can figure out what really happened . . ." His voice trailed off.

"I wish I knew. What does she know that she had to be silenced?"

"Guess!"

She looked at him. Her face was now perfectly serious. She shook her head.

"Try!" he insisted.

"I can't!"

"Why not? Is there something she would tell everyone about you, if you take up the issue of why she was doing this?"

Mariah was suddenly touched by a finger of ice. "Like what?"

"A mistake? Something that turned out to be bigger than you intended? Or uglier? Or that involved people you didn't intend to hurt?" He looked directly into her eyes. "And I'm talking about Sadie, not you."

She stared back at him. What had he heard about her? She could think of nothing particularly good. Gossip seldom was. But she was certain there were no indiscretions on Sadie's part, only cross words, an unkind gesture. With gossip, how much was supposition, deduction, or else simply taking the opportunity to be the center of attention? Gossip was almost always repeated, whether the story was accurate or not.

Oliver smiled, but it was reflective, even sad. "Some gossip is cruel, and some is relatively bland." He glanced down for a moment, as if considering something, then he looked back up at her. "When I first came to St. Helens, three years ago, there was a lot of curiosity as to who I was. Where did I come from? What was my profession? Where did I get my money, and how much did I have? Was there a woman in my life? If not, why not?"

Mariah winced. She was embarrassed for the women of the village. Of course, men could gossip, too, but she knew the source of this kind of thing was most often the women. She certainly had been guilty of it. In truth, her extreme distaste for it had come relatively recently.

"Ordinary, isn't it?" he said, and there was a sadness in his face now. "It happens almost anywhere, especially when you have people with too much time and too little purpose. I'm talking about something a good deal more powerful than that. In any case," he added. "I'll report only the things that she said to me."

Mariah drew in a sharp breath. "Sadie said . . . ?" She could only stare at him in anticipation.

"We all have things we would never want publicly

known," said Oliver. "It's hard to get over guilt, or grief, if we are constantly reminded of them. It's like putting a sticking plaster over a cut to keep it clean, and then making sure you don't knock it again and tear it open."

"I know," she said quietly. She understood in what he had already said that he, too, had his secrets, his privacies. "You don't—"

"Yes, I do. I raised the subject, so I must now finish it. When I was in North Africa, I chose a man to lead a command because I liked him and believed in him, and I did not like the alternative choice. I was wrong. The mission failed and it cost two men their lives. And more than that, the man I had promoted lost confidence in himself. If I had followed my intelligence information rather than my feelings, the mission might have succeeded, without loss of life. No one would have been disgraced."

She wanted to say something comforting, and then realized how automatic that was. Automatic and meaningless, as if she had not really been listening. So, she said nothing. Surely, he would know she had heard, and not only the words, but the meaning behind them.

A new thought suddenly occurred to her, an honest one. "Anyone who makes a decision risks making the wrong one. Is it better to decide nothing, and leave it to someone else who might do better? But then, they might not."

After a lengthy silence, Mariah was hit with a possibility. "Did Sadie know about what happened to you in North Africa?" What she didn't ask was the burning question: Was Sadie blackmailing Oliver Mallard? It was an inevitable conclusion, but one she could hardly grasp. She finally repeated this question to him and saw the color drain from his face. "How could she have known? She's never been anywhere near Africa."

Oliver released a loud sigh. "She learned it from a letter that she read. A letter that was stolen from the post office. She had no right to read it, but the information was correct, and any investigation would have substantiated the story. I could not deny it. To make it public would make my life in this village, which I value, very hard for me." His face was sad and, strong as it was, uniquely vulnerable.

"We all make mistakes," Mariah muttered quietly. "Some of us, like me, make the same mistakes over and over again. We tell ourselves we are the victims, and it's not our fault. We were justified. We couldn't help it. They deserve it. It would change something disastrously. All of which are lies. Not big ones, perhaps—not a lethal wound to anyone—more like having boils all over."

He smiled reluctantly. "You have a vivid imagination, Mariah."

"I've never had much of one," she admitted. "I had a very unhappy marriage and it turned me bitter and angry, so that I became intolerant, not only of my friends, but of my family. I was nasty, even hateful. I said things that cannot be forgotten, and which were completely unjustified, and I alienated everyone. At last, I could see that I was being excluded, that I would end my life alone, and it would be entirely my fault, not anyone else's. It took me a long time to see it and to do something about it. I can't undo any of it—I meant to hurt people and I did—but I can stop myself from doing it again."

"Did Sadie attack you over it?" he asked curiously.

That was a new thought. It had never occurred to her until this moment. Was that why Sadie had been so insistent that she come for this visit, because she finally intended to use Mariah's failings against her? And just as quickly as the question rose in her mind, the answer followed: no, it was not. Sadie had asked her to come because only Mariah would insist on looking for her. Only Mariah would be fearless in uncovering every aspect of her disappearance, and go on and on, until she was found. Did Sadie want her to do that? Why? It had to be more than her usual drama, her need to be the center of attention. Perhaps she meant to draw attention away from something else? But what?

"Did she say anything further to you about Africa?" she asked. "That she knew about it from reading someone else's letters? That's a crime, isn't it, to steal mail? She must have been very sure you wouldn't accuse her of that. What did you say to her?"

This time Oliver's smile was real. "She asked for money to keep silent and I told her to go to hell."

The wave of relief carried her high. In spite of the gravity of the situation, she was smiling widely. "Good," she exclaimed. "Very good!"

"Since you didn't ask," he continued, "I'll tell you everything. I don't know what has happened to her, or where she is. I told you about the blackmail because I don't know precisely who else she might have blackmailed, or tried to, but I'm certain I was not the only one. Why would she single out only me if it is in her nature to blackmail?"

Mariah frowned. "What did Sadie want? Was it just money? Information about someone she knew? I don't wish to intrude into private mistakes, griefs, even shame, but how could anyone recover, forgive, and move forward if everybody knows about whatever it is we are trying to conceal?" She sat with that thought for a moment. "But in this case, we need to know who her other victims were, in order to rescue her and stop a further tragedy." She looked steadily at Oliver. It was not easy, but she acknowledged to herself the importance of having a friend who liked her as she really was, and allowed her room to change, to repent and begin again, no matter how old she was.

"Thank you," he said earnestly. "We are lucky if we have long enough to get our errors acknowledged, and understand well enough to know what it is for which we are forgiven. The point just now is that I know what Sadie Alsop is really like, beneath the charm and occasional wit. What we need to do is rescue her and, even more important, at least to us, prevent whoever has her from doing damage that cannot be undone."

Mariah swallowed hard. "Like killing her? Even accidentally because they are afraid of what she will do to them?"

"Exactly. What we need to know is what she knows about other people. And I'm sorry that we need to pry, but it's the only way we can determine who else is vulnerable, and whether or not Sadie knew this. And if she did, did she use it? Threaten with it?" He stopped.

Mariah sensed there was a big glaring question he wanted to ask, like a massive hole in the road that was too wide to cross, caused by a deep crack in the earth.

They sat in silence, but Mariah's mind was whirring

with ideas. What was the relationship like between Sadie and Barton? Mariah had imagined in her own mind a story of horror, perhaps equal to that of her own marriage. But that could be a false parallel, created by her own shame. Oliver was giving her gentle encouragement to talk, if it might help. She remembered bits and pieces of the conversations with Sadie, especially those of thirty or forty years ago, when she had been desperate for someone to talk to. And it had to be someone outside her own family, or not acquainted with London society. It grew in her own mind, the pain. But, above all, there was the humiliation. She had always feared anyone knowing of her husband's abuse, and how they might visualize her on her hands and knees, naked, as her also naked husband inflicted such pain on her. No, she could not tell Oliver. In fact, she refused to put words to it at all, even in the dark hollows of her memories.

She looked up at Oliver and felt her face burn with shame. He should never know of this history. Not a word, not an idea. She could understand anyone confiding in Sadie at a time when they were in pain and too ashamed to bear it alone. But for Sadie to betray that trust? In Mariah's mind, this was as close to unforgivable as any human behavior could be.

She felt Oliver's eyes on her. Could she meet them?

She had as much reason as anyone, perhaps more, to wish Sadie silenced. She could even understand someone killing her if she had threatened to break their confidence and tell people. Oliver had faced her down when she had sneakily read a private letter, but who else in the village of St. Helens was a victim? It did not matter what their secret was. If it was a nightmare to the victim, although trifling to someone else, that would be enough. Was Sadie so drunk with her own power that she had not thought she was putting herself in danger? Perhaps not, if she had done this for years, and no one had fought back.

"Mariah," Oliver prompted gently, breaking her out of her thoughts, "I don't need to know what power she had over you. I only want to make sure, somehow, that short of killing her, she does not repeat it."

"If she has not already done so."

"We all have things to keep silent about," he remarked. "You may find judgment is a lot kinder than you expect."

Should she tell him? She forced herself to think of words for it. It would always be a lie between them, something she was too ashamed of to repeat. What might he guess? She closed her eyes. "My husband had unnatural tastes," she said in almost a whisper. "He treated me like an animal, beat me if I did not satisfy him. I was so ashamed. I did not have the courage to tell anyone. That's why I became bitter, and cruel, so no one could ever get close enough to me to know anything. My son, my only child, thought well of his father, and I didn't want to tarnish that. No," she quickly added, "that's a lie. It wasn't to preserve Edward's opinion of his father; it was that I could not bear my son to know about his pathetic mother."

She felt the tears run down her face, but it was pointless to try to dab at them with a small handkerchief.

"I never told anyone. I just grew angrier with everyone, because they didn't know. And I couldn't tell them. I blamed them for what they couldn't see. To everyone, he was an upright man who prayed to God, not a naked man beating his wife." She looked up at him and glared, as if he had forced the information out of her. "And to be honest," she added, "I might have been capable of doing terrible things to Sadie, if it meant stopping her from telling my family, my neighbors, even my grandchildren. But I never imagined that she would. I even thought that perhaps she was a victim of cruelty and humiliation, too, and she asked me here to help her, knowing what I had been through." She swallowed. "Isn't that absurd?"

"No," he replied quietly, but his voice shook a little. "You will always fight for a victim, even at the possible cost of your own privacy. I think that is extraordinarily brave. And now that this is out of the way, let's look into who else might have been a victim of this vicious woman. Much as I hate saying it, we may not have a great deal of time. She would have been all right in that house. It was warm enough, and she seems to have had food, but she's not there anymore. And it looks as if she's injured."

Mariah blinked away the last of her tears. She told herself they were self-indulgent, and she needed to get control. "She may already be dead. I think blackmail is a very wicked crime, and a victim might feel justified in torturing her to death. But that will not be how the law sees it." She took a deep breath before speaking the words that could reflect badly on her. "There is a part of me that really doesn't care if we save Sadie or not, but I do care that whoever has attacked her will answer for it. The law will have no mercy, whatever people might believe."

The moment those words were spoken, she wanted to take them back. "No, I do care, of course I do."

Oliver smiled softly, but it was a sad expression, far more than one of pleasure or amusement. "We have to work out who were Sadie's victims, and who became fed up with paying her, if money was involved. It would help to know. We have to consider that it may not have been money she was after."

"How can we do that?" she asked. "Those victims will hardly accuse her publicly. That would be as painful as Sadie telling everyone."

"Yes, I thought of that. We know a few things that might help us," he said. "She tried to get something from the people she blackmailed. She wanted money from me, but I have the feeling she would have demanded other things, if I had paid her."

"Did she try again?" Mariah interrupted. "That is, threaten to blackmail you?"

"No." Oliver looked a little awkward. "After I told her to go to hell, I said I could play the same game, and that gossip doesn't have to be true to do damage."

Mariah stared at him. "You—" She could not find the words whirling through her mind. What if he took offense, or questioned this new friendship? She felt foolish that it mattered.

He smiled bleakly. "I lost my temper. I don't think I could have actually spread rumors about her, but the mention of it worked."

"You think someone could have finally . . ." She did

not bother to finish this thought either. They both understood. "What do we do next? How do we find out who lashed back?"

"You believe it was one person, not more?" he asked.

"Yes," Mariah answered. "If I were the one doing something as dangerous as this, I wouldn't trust anyone else enough to tell them. I would work alone."

"I agree," he said quietly. "Whoever it is, whatever the secret, someone's prepared to risk their life to protect it. Tread softly, Mariah. Asking questions around the village might put you in danger. I realize you have no idea who is holding her, but they probably know that you are a longtime friend of Sadie's, and they might fear you are privy to some of their secrets. You must be very careful who you speak to. And also, above all, what you say."

"You think they would—" Her voice sounded perfectly normal, as if she were discussing a menu for dinner, but fear ran through her.

He turned the question around. "Don't you?"

"Yes." She had no doubt.

She saw how his shoulders relaxed a little, and he smiled.

"Then we will make a list," he told her. "And we'll work from it to exclude people, one by one, until we have only one left. We must be careful deciding who we can eliminate, and for what reason. We may not be able to do it without everyone knowing."

"Of course," she agreed. "We can say that we're trying to learn more about Sadie, so we can find out what happened to her. We can't be too delicate; her life is at risk."

Oliver nodded. "The first thing we need to do is inform Constable Hendershott. Now that you've discovered blood, this is no longer just a case of a missing person, Mariah. It could be attempted murder . . . or worse."

*M*ariah walked back slowly along the pavement, tired after her trip with Oliver to Bridgetown, to see the constable. The ice had melted to dirty water and was no longer slippery underfoot. Her head was in a whirl. Not of confusion, but of thoughts, ideas, and above all, resolve. There was no time to waste. Today there was a thaw, but the damp air was edged with ice all the same. Tonight, it would freeze again. These were the last two days before Christmas. And if Sadie was not found, and she was outside, or in an unheated place, there was no telling how long it would take before she froze to death.

Unless, of course, Sadie was not being held, although, without knowing why, Mariah believed that she was. And she was certain it was in St. Helens. St. Helens was where Sadie lived, where she knew people, their vulnerabilities, the things they valued. And most of the mistakes they had made. Someone local had her locked away, and they would not have gone far.

Mariah needed to start here, in the village, but how to proceed? And how did Sadie even know the secrets that people cared about, and deeply enough that they would submit, and go on submitting, to her threats? This was no time to be delicate.

Did the person behind this really want Sadie to die? Or had the whole plan to silence her got out of control? Maybe now the perpetrator was as frightened as Sadie herself. Instead of anger, Mariah felt pity for them. She felt sure it was a woman, someone who was not powerful. Mariah reminded herself that Sadie had even tried to pressure Oliver Mallard, and that had not worked, so she had backed away.

If Sadie had been home when Mariah arrived, would she have tried to poison Mariah's mind against Oliver? She would not have allowed it! Oliver had told her himself of his mistake, and the price he had paid. She had no way of knowing if it was true or not, but she wanted to believe him.

What swift-acting and insidious poisons were rumor and gossip!

Was Sadie doing this just for money? Or were there other things she accepted in pay, such as favors or small gifts?

What a lovely watch! You like it? I do, perhaps you would . . . ? Yes, of course, here it is. Thank you. Of course, I shall not mention the matter again. It will be our secret. Until next time I see that you have something I like!

And then there was *I made a mistake. You won't tell anyone, will you? Give me—and I shall not tell anyone what I know about your errors.*

That would work quite well. In fact, very well. No money to account for, just the favors, the small gifts. The discreet silences. Sadie would be invited to every party, whether she was welcome or not. Did anyone look at her new hat or piece of jewelry and wonder why she was always asked to every event?

Mariah turned the last corner and was on the road where Gwendolyn lived. She was glad to get inside, in the warmth. Gwendolyn had built up the fire, and

Mariah reminded herself that she must remember to help pay for such luxury. Discreetly, of course.

"Tea?" Gwendolyn offered immediately. "You look frozen." She gazed keenly at Mariah's face. "Did you learn anything?"

"Tea would be lovely," Mariah accepted with feeling. "And no, I didn't really learn anything, but I have a great many ideas. Chief among them is that we must find Sadie soon. We don't know her circumstances, the weather is bitter and it's going to snow before Christmas, which is only two days away. We have to help, whatever we think of her. Even if only for the sake of the person who took her. I don't believe they intended her to die, but this has got out of control."

She took off her hat and coat, then followed Gwendolyn into the kitchen, and watched her put the kettle on the hob. The kitchen was warm, and she ached to sit down and take the weight off her feet.

She set about helping Gwendolyn fetch out of the larder a cake and several small currant scones, on which Gwendolyn spread butter liberally. "It's Christmas" was the excuse she gave for such extravagance.

Mariah picked up the tray and carried it through before Gwendolyn could say anything about not being as good a cook as her sister, as she often did. Mariah did not know if it was true or not, and she did not care. Gwendolyn was warm and inviting, while Annabel was chilly and indifferent.

Mariah set the tray on the small table, and relaxed into what she had come to regard as her chair.

"What did you find out?" Gwendolyn asked, even before she had begun to pour the tea. Her face was alive with interest.

During most of the walk home, Mariah had been turning over the question of how much to tell Gwendolyn. She had reached no answer that satisfied her, but she could not afford to hold back now. "She's blackmailing people," she told her a little abruptly, but the shortness of temper was with herself, not Gwendolyn. "It looks as if one of her victims had come to the end of their patience." She looked at Gwendolyn's face and felt a stab of pity, but she had not allowed herself the choice of stopping. "I'm sorry. It is very ugly. It may have begun as something small—the observation of a weakness, an exhilarated knowledge because she was in the wrong place at the right time—it doesn't matter."

"Do you know this, or are you deducing it?" Gwendolyn asked. There was no anger in her voice, just unhappiness.

"I know it in one case; I suspect it in others. But there must be quite a few."

"Why? Why must there?"

"I don't have a good reason, but if you have succeeded at it, why would you stop when apparently you have the chance to continue?"

Gwendolyn shook her head sharply. "But it's—"

"Horrible," Mariah supplied for her. "But someone found her in the cottage and now they have taken her somewhere else, most likely against her own will. They cannot keep her forever so she must be in danger."

"Yes, I know," Gwendolyn said sharply. "But who would do that?"

"Someone she has made suffer more than they can take," Mariah replied. "No one could find it easy to live with the constant fear of having some tragic event in their lives exposed. To wake up every day with the fear that it will be today, and there is nothing that can make Sadie stop."

"Except to kill her," Gwendolyn finished the thought for her. "That's terrible. And what is even worse, I suppose, is that I think I can understand it. Fear makes you sick to your stomach, makes your head ache, keeps you from sleeping because it comes even into your dreams, and then you wake up sweating and cold at the same time."

Mariah stared at her curiously. She saw Gwendolyn blush.

"I was afraid of something once," Gwendolyn explained. "It happened, but it wasn't as terrible as I had expected. Still, I haven't forgotten how it felt." She glanced down at the fabric of her skirt. "It was painful, but it didn't last, not the way I was afraid it would. Now it's no more than embarrassing, but even embarrassment hurts."

"I know it does," Mariah said quite gently. She did not know the specifics, but she thought it had something to do with John, Gwendolyn's brother-in-law. Both sisters loved him, and he had chosen Annabel. No doubt before the wedding there had been many scenes Gwendolyn could not forget to this day, no matter how hard she tried. And Mariah did not find it difficult to believe that Annabel had seen and had perhaps made it harder. Or that John himself had been clumsy, although it had not seemed to be in his character. But some people are clumsy with words. Mariah had been often enough.

Gwendolyn was staring at her. Was she waiting for Mariah to say something painful, only too aware of Gwendolyn's dreams?

"It is up to us, I think, to find out who was blackmailed," Mariah went on. "But someone hates Sadie, and perhaps fears her enough to have put her through this ordeal. Perhaps it has gone further than was intended, and now they don't know how to stop it, before it ends in real tragedy."

"But if we find her alive, will she tell everybody who took her?" Gwendolyn said urgently. "She will want revenge. She won't be quiet about it for very long, you know?" Gwendolyn's face was furrowed with anxiety, and possibly behind it, not completely masked, a biting fear. Did she know who had abducted Sadie? Was there a darker side to Gwendolyn? Mariah looked at her now and could not believe this to be so.

But that was the point, wasn't it? Everyone has a hidden side. No one lives seventy or eighty years without a private pain, even if it is not so much a presence as an absence of something longed for and never possessed.

But it was pointless to speculate on how much Gwendolyn knew. "I do," Mariah replied. "But we can't sit here doing nothing and hoping. One of Sadie's blackmail victims is so afraid she will expose them that they have taken this terrible risk."

"Then their secret must be something frightful." Gwendolyn shook her head. "Terrible."

"Only terrible to them," Mariah corrected her. "We all have things we would very much prefer to forget. Possibly embarrassing rather than morally wrong. Certainly not criminal." She sat up a little straighter. "Now, let us stop posing questions and think of some answers. It won't help Sadie if we find out who has abducted her after she's dead!"

Gwendolyn shuddered. "Whoever it is will be so sorry! Sadie will destroy them. She doesn't forgive easily, you know."

"I wasn't thinking of forgiveness," Mariah argued. "I was thinking rather more of self-preservation. Knowing that she tried to blackmail her neighbors, Sadie has more need of forgiveness than anyone else. Don't forget that. I want to save her life, but I don't intend to let her forget what she has done."

"I wish you lived here," Gwendolyn whispered softly. "If you did, I would feel safer."

"Perhaps I will! I like that old cottage. I was thinking about it on the walk back here. I can think of all sorts of things to do in the garden." She stopped abruptly. What on earth was she saying? But if she sold her London house, she would have more than enough to buy the cottage and hire someone to clear and keep the garden. "Stop tempting me to be self-indulgent!" she exclaimed. "Now, how can we know who were Sadie's victims? What did she ask for? Money? I doubt it. Who has any to spare? A favor? Something of theirs she liked?"

Gwendolyn frowned. "That's what we need to know, but it's going to be difficult to discover."

"Of course, it is," Mariah agreed. "If it were easy, she would have been caught before now. No one is supposing Sadie is stupid, at least in the common-sense way. Think, please. There is no one else I can ask. And I certainly don't know." Another idea came to her. "What possessions in the village matter to people? You all care about your gardens. I remember that because in the summer they really are wonderful. Who's head of the Horticultural Society?"

Gwendolyn's eyes lit. "Sadie! It used to be Dorothy Costigan. She was very good, but Sadie is, too, of course. And now she is the president for life, so—"

"That matters," Mariah cut across her. "How did Dorothy let Sadie take over? Remember as exactly as you can. Don't assume anything."

"She had been president for several years, but suddenly she said she no longer wanted the responsibility. We gave her a rather special rosebush and thanked her."

"Who picked Sadie to replace her?"

"Well, she has a beautiful garden, you know? All spring and all summer it really is splendid."

"Sadie is the gardener? Or is it her husband?"

"Barton? No. It's actually John who does most of the regular work."

"John?" Mariah asked. "Why would Annabel's husband tend to Sadie's garden?"

"Just things like mowing the grass, moving the plants, splitting them up, that sort of thing," Gwendolyn explained. "And there's a little boy, one of the Wilsons, I think, who pulls weeds. But Sadie is very good about knowing what plants will flower where: in the sun or the shade, in what sort of soil, and that sort of thing. She knows a lot."

"But John does the work?"

"Yes, but don't read anything into that. John would never—" She stopped without finishing the sentence.

It wasn't necessary; Mariah knew what she was going to say, and neither of them knew if it was true. Was John being blackmailed, paying Sadie by working in her garden?

"Don't think about it," Mariah ordered, not sure if it would make any difference. They both understood how damaging suspicion could be. "You don't know if it's true. That is what's so poisonous: every kindness causes suspicion. She may even pay him. Or perhaps he's just kind?"

"With John, yes," Gwendolyn said quickly. "But it makes you doubt everything."

"What else?" Mariah asked. "Dorothy Costigan? Think of everything that changed the normal pattern."

"There was a brooch," Gwendolyn suggested. "A really beautiful one. I don't know that it was so expensive, but Dorothy loved it, and she gave it to Sadie, who wore it quite often. Of course, Dorothy said she had given it to Sadie as a gift, but there were tears in her eyes, and she wouldn't discuss it. I didn't like to ask her why she gave it away because it seemed intrusive. Should I have?"

"I don't think it would have helped," Mariah answered honestly. "It's done now. But do you have any idea what Dorothy could have to hide?" She swallowed hard and felt the discomfort ache in her body. "I wish I didn't have to do this. It makes every good act suspicious. It's a poison that infects everything it touches. That's one of the reasons a blackmailer gets away with it. Nobody knows who else it will hurt, perhaps even destroy."

"It's not even about the money, is it?" Gwendolyn went on. "It's not that she needs it. She just wants to—"

"Sadie is a very bitter and lost soul, if we are right," Mariah quickly said. "I'm sorry to include John, but we have to. Dorothy and Oliver, too. I think she intended to try it with me as well."

"You?" Gwendolyn stopped, as if not sure what to say, or how to say it.

"I've done some ugly things I would rather other people didn't know about. I regret them deeply. Not criminal, just . . . ugly."

"But she didn't use it against you?"

"Only because she isn't here," Mariah responded reasonably.

"Lizzie Putney takes her to the city about once a month, or thereabouts."

Mariah thought of the woman they had met in the tearoom. "I didn't think she liked Sadie. Are you saying that Lizzie does like her?"

"No," said Gwendolyn. "I mean that I think Lizzie could be another victim. She was afraid of Sadie."

"Can you see any one of those people doing this to her?"

Gwendolyn shook her head. "Do you think we should ask Annabel? She's very clever, you know. Much quicker than I am." She smiled apologetically. "She might notice things I didn't, and she doesn't gossip."

Mariah drew in her breath to refuse. If John was a victim, and Gwendolyn had always cared for him, would she protect him? Whatever she intended, she had to be deeply involved emotionally. Whatever John had done, or Sadie thought he had done, would hurt Gwendolyn. But what would not hurt her? Her fears for him, and for Annabel, would fill in all spaces with whatever she wanted or needed to believe.

"Mariah?" Gwendolyn pressed urgently.

"Yes, of course," Mariah replied. "We must include your sister, but carefully. There are things we mustn't share, if we don't have to. That would be almost worse than what Sadie is doing. We'll go and see Annabel. And John, of course."

*A*s it turned out, Mariah and Gwendolyn were invited to John and Annabel's house for an early dinner. It was dusk by four in the afternoon, and a freeze had set in, the ice on the pavement smooth and slick. It was wise to wear thick rubber-soled boots, and to take each other by the arm and tread carefully. The sky was completely overcast, and the slicing wind whipped along the bare branches of the trees close to the road.

They walked slowly. A fall could be very bad. They both knew it and made no excuses for extra care. It was a relief to them to reach Annabel's house and make their way safely up the path.

Gwendolyn was reaching for the doorbell when the door swung open and John welcomed them inside.

"How are you?" he asked, looking from one of them to the other. "It's going to be a hard night. Come in and get warm. Hot lamb stew for dinner, with onions and white turnips, and a little drop or two of wine in the stew."

"Perfect," Mariah said sincerely with a smile.

He flashed a smile back at her, then at Gwendolyn.

Mariah saw the faint color in Gwendolyn's cheeks deepen.

The meal was excellent, as Mariah had expected it to be. Annabel had every reason to be proud of her cooking. The whole house was warm, the colors were comfortable, nothing overpowering or clashing, and yet it did not have the air of peace that Mariah felt in Gwendolyn's much more modest house. Or perhaps it was just a different kind of ease?

They spoke casually, the conversation polite and inconsequential, all of them carefully skirting the subject of Sadie and her disappearance. It changed when Gwendolyn pointed to the mantelpiece. "Where's the photograph of Mother? Did you break the glass?"

"No," John answered.

"Yes," Annabel said at the same moment.

Neither looked at the other.

Mariah wondered what Annabel knew about John's gardening work for Sadie. Was she afraid that he was involved in Sadie's disappearance and that she had to protect him? Did he know where Sadie was now?

Gwendolyn's face crumpled in confusion. She turned from Annabel to John, and then back again. "The one in the silver frame," she elaborated.

"We have only one photograph of her," Annabel replied quietly. "It fell on the floor and the glass broke. We'll get it mended."

John looked a trifle startled and confused.

"The silver frame?" Mariah asked, then saw Annabel's face and instantly wished she had kept her own counsel. The picture was of Gwendolyn and Annabel's mother, and of no value to anyone else.

The silence remained, bristling and yawning— empty.

Mariah scrambled for something, anything to say that would help, and found nothing.

At last, it was Annabel who spoke. Her face was white, and her voice was slightly unsteady. "You are right. It is the silver frame. It was worth quite a lot. I gave it to Sadie, to keep her silence."

No one moved. It was the answer Mariah had dreaded, and yet her only feeling was surprise that Annabel admitted to being one of Sadie's victims. What should she say? She needed to know the truth, but did she want it at this price? Her instinct was to excuse herself. She was not part of this family. And yet she would not escape responsibility for the whole octopus-like thing in their midst, its tentacles encircled around an unknown number of people. No one could escape responsibility for what they did or did not do.

But it was Gwendolyn who broke the silence.

"You paid Sadie? With the silver frame, but for . . . ?" She did not finish the sentence; the rest of the question hung in the air.

Annabel's eyes moved from one to the other of them, except she did not look at her husband. "This is a small village. It is my home. I live here and I want to stay. I will not be driven out by everyone's gossiping neighbor, every old woman swapping stories at the greengrocer's, little children coming out of the schoolyard looking at us and giggling, and my imagination picturing what they are saying, what they think they know."

"But, what . . . ?" Gwendolyn began, and then stopped. She might just as well have completed her question. They all knew what the rest of it had to be.

Mariah asked the practical question. "What guarantee have you that she will not repeat it, whatever it is? Or keep asking for more?"

"I told her that if she asked for more, I would tell everyone why I gave it to her. She's done it to others. If it becomes public, she is finished."

Gwendolyn looked both sad and confused. "But you couldn't prove it. The police wouldn't—"

Annabel cut across her. "Not the police, for heaven's sake! The other people in the village. We don't know who else she was blackmailing! If you drive people too far, and you have already taken from them what you wish, you have created a very dangerous enemy for yourself."

Mariah glanced between them all. Annabel was pale but composed. Gwendolyn was clearly both frightened and confused. John looked appallingly miserable, but Mariah did not know what it was precisely that distressed him so much, or even if it surprised him. Mariah herself tried to control her expression and not reveal what she had deduced.

Gwendolyn opened her mouth to speak, and then closed it, clearly not knowing what to say.

It was Annabel who broke the silence. "I would have exposed her, and she knows it," she said, her voice strong with conviction. "It seems someone else has chosen a different path." She turned toward Mariah specifically, as if addressing her alone. "So please, do not dig into this any further, for the sake of everybody. I don't know how many others she's done this to. Most of us have things we would rather were not gossiped about, or didn't wonder what the laughter was about, and why the sudden silence when we came into the room. You will make no friends by exposing us all. One of the secrets may be darker than even Sadie could guess and has led to her downfall."

"I know that," Mariah whispered quietly. "And I hope this experience has taught Sadie the danger of what she's been doing, if not the wickedness. But the law will not find it an adequate excuse for her death, if her body is found. And if she is not rescued soon, it may be too late."

Surprisingly, it was not Annabel who replied, or even John, in her defense; it was Gwendolyn. "If Annabel knew where Sadie was, she would tell us," she told Mariah confidently.

Mariah kept her voice as level as she could, but it wavered slightly all the same. "Even if it were to protect John?"

John stared at Annabel, who was looking at Gwendolyn. When John spoke, his voice was low, yet every word fell upon absolute silence from everyone else. "I would rather have the whole village talking about me and my family than to have caused Sadie's death over it. She was blackmailing me, and Annabel paid her with the silver frame. Whether that would be enough, or not, we don't know. But if not, then the fact that we paid would be enough to ruin her. And before your imagination runs riot, my sin was seriously wrong, but not criminal." He hesitated only a moment. Perhaps no one noticed it except Mariah. "But my wife forgives me, and it is no one else's business."

Mariah did not guess what his offense might have been. From John's embarrassment, and the way he had phrased his admission, it was clear enough that his offense was against Annabel. One answer presented itself: he had had an affair, since his marriage, and she had chosen to forgive him. That lay between them. But it would be almost impossible to live with had it been made public. No wonder he had paid Sadie! And Annabel would keep it secret, for her own sake.

Mariah's dislike, even loathing, for Sadie hardened like a bitter lump inside her. "I see," she replied with total clarity. "Sadie is a wicked woman, but we must not sink to the depths of letting her die."

"Of course you are right," John agreed.

Beside him, Annabel nodded silently.

*M*ariah and Gwendolyn walked most of the way back home in silence. It was a long time before Mariah decided to speak. "You find it hard to forgive," she said, more of a conclusion than a question.

Gwendolyn took a deep breath, and then let it out without answering.

"You thought he was better than that," Mariah continued.

"It must have hurt Annabel terribly," Gwendolyn responded, shaking her head in disbelief. "She is very strong, I know, but that doesn't mean she isn't horribly . . ." She could not finish the sentence, as if saying it would make it a reality.

"You don't know what happened," Mariah pointed out.

Gwendolyn stopped and turned to look at Mariah. "Did you see her face? The pain in it. And he admitted it quite openly!"

"Yes," Mariah agreed. "Nor did he make any excuses. I admire him for that. He didn't blame her for being . . . cold, or—"

"You don't know that she was," Gwendolyn protested.

"No, and neither do you," Mariah countered. "But just because he didn't say it does not mean it isn't true. If you want to have any relationship that works, you have to forgive, just as you would hope to be forgiven."

"But I would never . . ." Gwendolyn argued.

"Oh, no?" Mariah raised her eyebrows. "You seem

very sure of that. Not even if you were married to someone who criticized you, even in front of others? Never gave you any affection?"

"John isn't—" Gwendolyn looked confused. "Oh, you mean Annabel?"

"I mean anyone at all," Mariah replied. "We don't know what goes on between other people. And it isn't any of our business. If Annabel can forgive him, and it appears she has, then why can you not? Because he doesn't live up to your ideal of what you imagined him to be? What do you want to do? Hold it against him forever, so Annabel is constantly reminded of it?"

"No!"

"Are you sure? It really isn't anyone else's business, you know. Relationships are complicated. And we all need to be forgiven, have the past forgotten, some time or other."

"Did you . . . ?" Gwendolyn began.

"Forgive? Some things. Not everything," Mariah replied honestly. "And if you expect me to tell you about it, you are mistaken. Some wounds cannot heal, even a little bit, if you keep remembering them. You need to forgive for your own sake, if not for theirs. I learned that from my own life. And I have no intention of living the traumas again to assuage your curiosity."

"I didn't ask!"

"I know you didn't," Mariah said gently. "As for John, he did not give any excuses, although I imagine there might be many. That is very much to his credit. This fault is not yours to forgive, or not to. And if you make it so, you will be making it impossible for Annabel to get over it. Or is that what you want?"

"Of course not!"

"Then put it out of your mind. We have far more important things to do."

"I know."

"Do you? Do you realize that if we do not find Sadie in the next few hours, it will be Christmas Eve, and I fear too late. In fact, we might already be too late."

"But—"

"Perhaps not," Mariah said, a lift of hope in her voice that she did not feel. "We must think. Someone took Sadie from the cottage. Dorothy may be one of Sadie's victims. Have you any idea why?"

"No. I mean, she's a gossip. If that's something over which to be blackmailed, half the women in the village would be victims."

"What do you know about her?" It was a futile question, and she realized it as soon as the words were out of her mouth.

"Well, when Dorothy was head of the Horticultural

Society," Gwendolyn told her tentatively, her face pensive and uncertain, "she was good at it. She gave everyone encouragement, even in the oddest things. We liked that. And she had all sorts of knowledge. She would come to your garden and suggest things that would work. She knew how to rearrange plants so they all looked better. She knew what kind of soil each plant liked."

"You told me that Sadie took over her position, but why?" Mariah prompted.

"I only know that Dorothy resigned, and Sadie took over."

"I see." And yet there was something she did not see, and she needed to. She was getting desperate. There was so little time left, and she was convinced she was trying to save a blackmail victim from committing murder. She had a growing conviction that any resolution had been taken from her hands, by circumstances out of her control. If there was a puppeteer pulling strings, she had no idea who that could be. "What else do you know about Dorothy? And is there a Mr. Costigan? Any children?"

"No children, and I think she's a widow. One doesn't like to ask. He may not be dead, but just not here. Or maybe he never existed."

"Is that worth blackmailing over? An invented husband? Surely not. It seems more a domestic tragedy than anything worthy of blackmail." Mariah felt more and more useless. They knew so much, and yet so little that made sense.

They walked together along the last stretch of pavement to Gwendolyn's house.

It was warm inside. Mariah was feeling more and more at home in this house. It was probably worth half of what Annabel's would fetch. Little in it was new, but it was all, in its way, uniquely comfortable and inviting.

They went into the kitchen, warming themselves from the freezing outside air by sitting near to the stove. Gwendolyn made hot chocolate, which they drank slowly, and each ate a couple of chocolate biscuits.

"We can't afford to wait until the answer comes to us," Mariah said quietly. "There's still time to do something. At least, I hope there is. You said that Dorothy gave Sadie her favorite brooch, and yet she doesn't like her."

"Yes, that's true."

"I'm not very good at being diplomatic," Mariah went on. "And there isn't any time for it now."

Gwendolyn shivered. "But what can we do? You're

clever, and I don't think you're afraid of anything! You would never run away, but there is still the answer to find."

Mariah had the words of denial on her tongue, but right now Gwendolyn needed her to be whatever she believed. Without hesitation, she had offered Mariah her hospitality, and made her welcome. Mariah had no alternative but to do her best to achieve what Gwendolyn wished, hoped for, and what the village needed. "It is not a matter of never running away," she told her. "It is that we must attack, find the truth, and force it into the open. Blackmail is a kind of poison. I don't want anybody's secrets posted in the Market Square. They aren't ours to expose. And while it might remove Sadie's power, at what cost?"

"Can't we get together and agree to stop the gossip and backbiting?" Gwendolyn cried tentatively.

"Yes. I think we can," Mariah replied slowly. "If we were to . . ." She took a deep breath. "Starting tomorrow morning."

"Do you have a plan?"

"Not now, but I might have, by the time we wake up."

Once warm in bed, Mariah had intended to be awake till she did have a good plan, but she was exhausted, emotionally and physically, and bereft of ideas. She calmed herself with thinking about the cottage in Briar Lane, what she could make of it if it were hers. However, questions about Sadie rolled around in her mind while she was dreaming, but no solutions came.

*W*hen she awoke in the morning, Mariah felt energized and determined to solve this problem, even if she made a fool of herself and was never invited back to St. Helens. And, yes, even if the resolutions were not happy ones. If it turned into a tragedy, it was far better to face it than to run away, or pretend that they had done their best when they had not. She knew better than most that there were secrets best not known. This was not one of them.

Mariah washed, and dressed warmly. When she went down to the kitchen, she was not surprised to find Gwendolyn already there, as she had been every morning. Mariah stood in the doorway, watching her new friend move about, putting dishes away, folding a tablecloth. Gwendolyn was so deep in concentration that she did not notice Mariah, who thought this was probably indicative of how troubled she was.

Mariah pulled the door wider and the movement caught Gwendolyn's eye. She looked up and quickly changed her expression to a smile. "Good morning. How are you? Did you sleep well?" There was a lift in her voice.

Mariah thought that she must be making a tremendous effort. She stepped into the room. "I slept very well, thank you," she replied. "And I have made up my mind what I will do, at least to begin with." She hesitated a moment. "That is, unless you disagree, of course."

Gwendolyn stood still for a moment, the teapot in one hand, the kettle on the stove beginning to steam. She pulled if off the hob. "What have you decided?" she asked.

"We must get one of the blackmailed people on our side."

Gwendolyn swallowed. "Not Annabel or John?"

Mariah noticed that she included Annabel, although according to both Annabel and John, it was he who had been the victim. Mariah had wondered at the time if there was more to the story, but she had no need to pursue it. That is, not yet. "No," she replied. "They will defend each other, which is natural. And it would place you in a very awkward position."

Gwendolyn stiffened. "I would not countenance blackmail, even if my own family was involved." Her voice was low, and a bit shaky.

"I would not place you in that position. Besides, we really do need people unrelated to each other." Mariah swallowed. "Sadie tried to blackmail Oliver, too, but he would not yield. But then, none of his family was involved. In fact, I don't know if he has any family. But Dorothy is vulnerable, alone, and has a need to be accepted. The perfect victim. And you said she gave Sadie her favorite brooch, as well as leadership of the gardening community."

Gwendolyn let out a shaky breath. "What can I do to help?"

"You've done it already. Think of all the other things that might be relevant. And don't speak to Annabel about it." She immediately wondered if she should have said that. "I don't want her to think that we feel strongly about what she told us. Better to behave as if we have forgotten it. After all, it is not our concern."

"I agree. I would like to believe I hadn't heard it."

"Very wise," Mariah agreed with feeling. "What can I do to help with breakfast?"

"It's a very cold day. What about bacon and eggs, and then toast and marmalade? And tea, of course."

"Perfect," Mariah replied with an easy smile.

Gwendolyn offered a smile in return, and Mariah thought it was with uncertainty, but it quickly became warm, sincere. "I like having you here for Christmas," she told her earnestly, and then blushing slightly, she turned to warming the teapot.

*M*ariah walked briskly to Dorothy Costigan's house, which she recognized straightaway, thanks to Gwendolyn's directions. The shapes of the flowerbeds in the large front garden and the splendid rose hedge made it markedly different from its neighbors. In Mariah's eyes, it was a gardener's joy: laid out well, soil dark and rich, and everything trimmed or pruned and ready for the spring. She remembered that this was the woman whose pride it was to be head of the Horticultural Society. That is, until Sadie replaced her.

She walked up the path and knocked on the front door. She waited for several moments and was about to turn away when the door opened.

It was a moment before Dorothy recognized Mariah, and then she smiled a little nervously.

"Good morning," Mariah said with an answering smile. "I've come to ask for your help."

The woman's smile eased. "Of course, anything I can do. Please come in." She opened the door more widely and stepped back.

Mariah followed her in, closing the door behind her.

"I hope the kitchen is all right," Dorothy said politely. "I haven't lit the fire in the sitting room yet." She stopped, as if this was a question.

"Perfect," Mariah replied. "Kitchens are always warm, and usually full of inviting aromas. I see that yours faces the morning sun. How pleasant." She glanced around appreciatively. She would have done that whatever had been the light, but the praise was sincere.

"Thank you." Dorothy was clearly pleased. "Would you like a cup of tea?"

"No, thank you," Mariah declared. "I slept late and have only just had breakfast. But it is kind of you to offer, especially because I have called without asking your approval."

"It must be important." She offered Mariah one of the kitchen chairs and took another for herself. "What can I do for you?"

Mariah felt guilty. There was no fear in the woman's

face, only pleasure at having the opportunity to help. She had to take a deep breath and think of the brooch the woman had forfeited, perhaps a gift from her dead husband.

"Sadie asked me here for Christmas," she began. "We used to be friends many years ago, in our youth, and this is a very pleasant village to stay in over a holiday. At first, I did not consider it anything other than a visit of a few days, recalling old memories, and that kind of thing."

She saw the confusion in the woman's face. She must come to the point. She seized on a lie that would explain what she was going to say. "But now I have considered my past visits, and something Barton said made me worried that Sadie . . ." She took a deep breath. "Now that she has disappeared and I had at first taxed Barton with it, somewhat roughly, I admit, I now think he does not know where she is any more than I do. But he made one or two remarks that I found disturbing." She gritted her teeth and looked straight into Dorothy Costigan's eyes, and then lowered her own gaze. "There are certain things in my past that I deeply regret. I will tell you if it is necessary, but I am profoundly ashamed of them." She looked up at Dorothy's face, which was now troubled and full of pity. "Not criminal, you understand, just embarrassing. No, humiliating. Sadie and I have known each other for many years, and I felt a closeness to her, which is the reason I confided my troubles to her. I think she half guessed my secret, for her expression implied she had suffered similarly. But I now realize that this was not the case. She hadn't suffered the same, but by pretending was merely encouraging me to confide in her. Then, when I told her the truth, she was prepared to hold my humiliating secret over my head."

Dorothy said nothing, but the pity in her face betrayed a total understanding.

"I am afraid that when she comes back from wherever she is, she will ask of me things I am not willing to do," Mariah continued. "I would rather face the scorn of the village than give in to her." She glanced at Dorothy, then away again. It was only too obvious in the woman's eyes that she understood perfectly. The word *blackmail* did not need to be spoken.

The silence grew heavy.

In the end, it was Dorothy who broke it. "What can I do? She's . . ." She was unable to finish.

"She's doing this to a lot of people," Mariah finished for her. "If we stand together and find her before it is too late—if it's not too late already—we will tell her that none of us will ever pay her again, whatever it is she wants. At the moment, we know of no crime against her, only her crime against us. And if we stand together, she will find herself ostracized. No one will speak to her. The shops will ask her to leave, and the local societies will no longer accept her membership."

The moment Mariah spoke, she heard her own words. Harsh, almost cruel. She wondered if this is the price we pay when we harbor such anger.

Dorothy shook her head. "They won't deny her; she has influence," she said in little more than a whisper.

"But it's limited," Mariah argued. "She must have her own secrets, too. I don't know them, and I don't want to, but before I give her another thing, I will tell people what she has done."

She saw the shadow cross Dorothy's face and she was touched by this. "I don't mean to sound cruel," Mariah said. "If I've learned one thing, it's that forgiveness is important. Even if Sadie is unrepentant, we must be forgiving." She bit her lip till it hurt. "And if we don't find her, if we let her die, then we will have a secret far worse than any of hers. We will never be rid of it!" She stopped and waited. "Is your secret so terrible you'd let Sadie die for it?" she asked gently.

Dorothy got up and walked quietly out of the room.

Mariah waited. The kitchen was warm, but she felt like ice inside her clothes, and yet her body was sweating.

Dorothy came back with a small photograph, unframed. She handed it to Mariah, who took it and looked at it. It was of a child, a little girl of about five or six. Her face was unusual, not quite properly formed, and her smile was wide, but there was a peculiar vacancy in her eyes.

"My daughter," Dorothy whispered. Her voice choked into a sob, instantly smothered. "Her name is Jenny."

For a moment, Mariah was silenced with pity, and then she mentally kicked herself. There was no time for her own feelings. They were less than nothing, in comparison to Dorothy's. She looked straight back at the woman, meeting her eyes.

Dorothy was staring at her, the tears running down her cheeks. "My husband couldn't live with it. He said it was my fault, something I did when I was carrying her. There's no one like that in his family. After she was born, he walked out, and then he divorced me." When Mariah said nothing, Dorothy took a deep breath, as if to gain courage. "He went to court—or to some friend who could pull strings—and he had his name removed from the birth certificate. I was so defeated, and he convinced me that I couldn't manage alone, so I sent Jenny away to be looked after."

"You don't have to explain yourself to me," Mariah told her. "I will defend your daughter, Jenny, if anyone is wicked enough to say something cruel."

"Thank you," Dorothy mumbled through her tears. "But you won't be here. You've no idea."

"I will," Mariah promised immediately. "I'm going to buy that cottage that is for sale. I am tired of London. I can always take the train back, if I want a day out. Both of my grandchildren are married and live there. But I shall make my home here. And Sadie knows me better than to imagine she can push me around or silence me." She took a deep breath, realizing what she had just said. But it gave her a feeling of certainty, assurance. She would move here. She would stand up against Sadie. Perhaps Sadie's husband, Barton Alsop, also needed defending. Sadie seemed to be a woman of infinite cruelty. But Mariah was not afraid of her, because she was not afraid of the memories inside herself any longer. She would attack Sadie if she was still alive and could be found, rescued, and then accused. She would defend Dorothy from public scorn all she could, and she would not back down. It was easier for Mariah because she did not have to stay in St. Helens. She would live here by choice.

She glanced at Dorothy. The woman was looking at Mariah with amazement, and a sudden flare of hope.

*M*ariah had no doubt as to what must be her next step, and that was to enlist the help of Oliver. She realized it might mean exposing the secret he had shared with her without hesitation, yet definitely with shame. Mariah needed the names of all those Sadie had blackmailed. It might not be easy. No one wanted their neighbors, the postman, the greengrocer, the boy who delivered the milk, to know their intimate secrets, the things they were most ashamed of, and most embarrassed by. It was their shame that gave Sadie her power. Without it, she was simply a spiteful and unhappy woman willing to hurt others for her own gain and, in some cases, self-aggrandizement. That, too, was indeed something vulnerable, and to be ashamed of, but Sadie seemed not to recognize her own vulnerabilities. Most of the secrets she held concerned acts from the past, irreversible now. Sadie knew how to exploit them and drag these sins and misdeeds into the present. And if no one stood up to her, the exploitation would continue indefinitely. Mariah must remember that, whenever her resolve weakened.

She walked to the bookshop in the high street, hoping Oliver would be there. If not, she would have to wait for him, or if that proved too long, find him wherever he was. It was Christmas Eve, and bitterly cold. The sky was overcast. It might well snow before nightfall. Sadie might not live through the night. Of course, she might be dead already! But the matter must be faced, for everyone else's sake. And for hers, too.

It was with overwhelming relief that she reached the bookshop and saw the lights were on, and the "Open" sign faced outward. She went straight in, and the little bell over the door rang a cheerful welcome. She was not so certain that Oliver would consider her welcome when she told him what she had done. Without mentioning it to him, she had just told Dorothy that she intended to buy the cottage and move to St. Helens! What on earth had possessed her to do that?

She closed the door behind her, considered for a moment turning round the notice that said "Open," then thought that would be an impertinence.

Oliver appeared at the far side of the room, which was cluttered with its usual books, papers, pens, and the tools for mending book spines in states of disrepair or neglect. He smiled when he saw her, although she thought it possible that he smiled at everyone who came into the shop.

He drew in breath, possibly to ask her how she was, and then looked at her face, and seemed to change his mind. "What has happened?" he asked.

She walked over to one of the chairs and sat down. She had not realized until now how tired her feet were, and her legs. She had already walked at least two miles on the icy pavement this day.

He sat down on the bench on the far side of the worktable, his expression still one of acute attention.

"I have discovered other people who were Sadie's victims," she began. "John Spears and, I think, his wife, Annabel. And we know about you, and I believe Sadie fully intended to blackmail me, only she disappeared before I arrived. That is four people, Oliver. But this morning, I discovered number five." Suddenly, her voice was choked with tears. This was absurd! Dorothy did not want pity. What she needed was practical help, and encouragement to fetch her child out of care and bring her home to her mother, and a village that would befriend her.

Oliver waited.

Mariah swallowed hard. "She is blackmailing Dorothy Costigan over the disabilities of her only child. The girl lives in an institution because she is not only mentally disabled, but physically different as well."

Oliver's face showed shock, pity, and then a deep and consuming anger.

"I see you feel as I do," Mariah assured him with a sudden upsurge of emotion. "Dorothy needs to bring the child home, to a village that will treat her kindly. She may be severely handicapped, but she needs to be loved, above all by someone who loves her as she is. Dorothy needs to do that, otherwise she cannot live comfortably with herself."

"Of course," he agreed at once. "And Sadie needs to be forgiven, although if what you have just said is indeed true, I'm not sure if I can do that. That is a lot to ask of anyone."

"We all need to be forgiven; the size of the sin is irrelevant," Mariah said with conviction. "This is Christmas Eve, a very good time to realize that the forgiveness of sin is ultimately God's business, but it starts with us. Whoever took her, whatever their weakness that Sadie used to her own advantage, letting her die will only make matters worse. As soon as it becomes a police matter, we will all be investigated and there will be no secrets left. Someone will go to prison or . . ." She could not finish the thought. Looking at Oliver's face, she knew he understood.

"We must find her," he declared. "We must look until

we do. We have to know what happened to her, not to punish the guilty so much as to exonerate the innocent. And if she is still alive, to save her, at least from death. How much she can be saved from guilt is up to her."

"And to us," Mariah added. "We must be saved from the further guilt of cruelty equal to hers. I don't want to be equal to Sadie Alsop, I want to be better. I want to say that I had a second chance, and I took it."

Oliver smiled with a curiously soft and lopsided expression. "And do you believe that everyone else is going to feel the same?"

She didn't suppose it for a moment. "I must give them the chance. I am ashamed of the way I used to be, and I want to be rid of all that badness."

"You are a brave woman, Mariah." His voice was suddenly soft.

"No, I'm not. I've just learned a little sooner than some," she replied.

"Then learn to leave me my own judgment."

She looked at him, and saw in his face a considerable gentleness that was too honest to lie, however kindly. Self-consciously, and feeling the heat rise up her face, she accepted it, then continued with the job at hand, which felt increasingly urgent, this close to Christmas, when attention would wander from Sadie

Alsop and her disappearance. "We must organize the village to look for her. The person who knows where to find Sadie is extremely unlikely to tell us, but we need to get to Sadie first, before . . ." She stopped. Her throat seemed to close up so she could not draw breath to say the words.

"Yes, I see what you mean. If everyone knows we're looking for Sadie, the person who's holding her prisoner can't risk having her found alive. Which also means that our looking for her could be dangerous for us."

Mariah thought about this for a moment. "It seems that the safest course is sending out people—the search party—in threes. With two, if one of them is the culprit, the second would need to be silenced. Yes," she said, almost to herself, "we'll go out in threes."

"That makes sense," Oliver replied. "But no more than three, because we won't be able to cover as much ground before dark. Heaven knows, it's often dark by four, this time of the year. Earlier, if the clouds close in and it snows."

"Then we must start now," Mariah insisted. "How do we get people from the village to join us? To raise a search party will take all day if we do no more than knock on doors."

"Ring the church bells!" Oliver's eyes became brighter.

"As they did in medieval times. I'll ask the vicar to ring the ancient alarm, or at least something different from any of the usual carillons. Word will spread quickly! All we need are fifty or sixty people, divided into groups of three."

"Yes!" Mariah agreed. "Will you ask the vicar now?"

"*We* will ask him now," he replied, rising to his feet.

Mariah opened her mouth to protest, and then closed it. There was nothing to say. It was time to keep promises.

$\mathcal{I}$t took twenty minutes for Oliver to collect his heavy jacket and his calf-high winter boots, the ones fit for walking through deep snow and, occasionally, even deeper drifts and rougher ground. He also brought a hat and two scarves, one for himself, the other for Mariah.

"Thank you," she said soberly, taking off the hat that covered her head, but not her ears or neck. She might look ridiculous, but it had never mattered less. She was already wearing fur-lined leather gloves.

They set out together. The air smelled of snow.

They bent into the wind and cold as they walked down the high street, turning onto the road that passed in front of the church. In the traditional way, the vicar's house was next door to it.

They walked up to the porch without hesitating. All the decisions were made. Oliver rang the doorbell and stepped back. He glanced at Mariah but said nothing.

She nodded.

He was about to reach for the bell again when the door opened, and the mild face of the vicar peered out. He looked faintly puzzled as he glanced first at Oliver and then at Mariah. "Yes?"

"We need to speak to you, Mr. Wilkinson," Oliver replied urgently. "May we come in?"

"It's Christmas Eve!" the man protested. "I'm preparing my sermon for the Watch Night service, and—"

"Sadie Alsop is still missing," Oliver interrupted. "She may already be dead."

"Aren't you being a little extreme? I'm sure—"

"What?" Oliver said quite softly, but his face was set in hard lines.

Mariah was certain that if the vicar were paying attention, he would not have begun an argument.

"Mr. Wilkinson, do you know where Mrs. Alsop is? And that she is alive and well?"

The vicar stared at Oliver for a moment. "Er, no, I don't know, but—"

"Then we must come in!" exclaimed Oliver, his hand lightly on Mariah's arm, as if including her in the request so the vicar would have to answer to them both.

Wilkinson hesitated.

"If Sadie Alsop dies because we did not look for her, but went to church to listen to a sermon instead, it will be a Christmas the people of St. Helens will never forget."

"Aren't you being a little melodramatic?" the vicar asked with a frown.

Mariah drew in her breath, glanced at Oliver, then addressed the man. "Mr. Wilkinson, Sadie has been missing for five days now, and we have done a certain amount of work trying to learn where she went. One thing we discovered is that she has been blackmailing several people in the village, not just . . ."

"Not just the two of us," Oliver filled in.

The color drained from the vicar's face. "You? I think you should—"

"Mr. Wilkinson," said Oliver tartly, "it is not my imagination that she attempted to blackmail me, or several others in the village. It is quite possible that one or more of Sadie Alsop's victims has kidnapped her and left her somewhere. And now they will be afraid that we will rescue her, and she would retaliate by telling all their secrets: weaknesses, tragedies, mistakes, anything they do not wish to make public."

"Really, you're being a little hysterical, Mr. Mallard."

"Can you afford to wait any longer to look for her?" Oliver asked. "I won't rest till I have tried to find her. I think most of the village will feel as we do."

The vicar swallowed. "Blackmail, you say? Are you sure?"

"Yes," Oliver replied. "She tried to extort money from me. I told her to go to hell, and that I have no problem helping her to get there."

"There? What are you talking about? Did you take—"

"I'm talking about hell, Mr. Wilkinson. And no, she'll get there all by herself. I didn't know, at the time, that there were many other people she had tried to black-mail, and in some cases had succeeded."

The vicar shook his head, but the resistance was gone from his face. "Who else have you informed of this situation?"

For the first time, Mariah intruded. "If you ring the correct toll on the bells, Mr. Wilkinson, the people will hear, and they will know that it is an emergency. In the past, the church was the haven for all of us. If we were under attack, we found shelter there. It was the heart of joy, safety, comfort in times of grief. If we are not together over this—if you are not with us—then we are not together at all. A church leader who will not ring the bells to get everyone to come and save a life does not have the right to gather us together for anything, and that includes praising God."

The vicar looked at Oliver, as if waiting for him to argue against Mariah's accusations, but he saw only agreement.

"Perhaps you are right," he conceded. "If it is unnecessary, and I pray it is, I will apologize, but it would be better than the tragedy you suggest. I will ring the bells. I would like you to be beside me when I explain this to our townspeople."

"Of course," Oliver agreed. "Mariah and I will be there. But first we must tell them the facts, which you do not know for yourself . . . and it would be unfair to expect you to know."

The vicar did not argue. Mariah thought he looked relieved, having such a great responsibility removed from his hands.

The dining-room door opened and Wilkinson's wife came into the hall. She looked at her husband. "For heaven's sake, Oswald, invite them to sit and offer them tea! It's perishing outside, and by leaving the door open you are making the whole house cold." She turned to Mariah. "Mrs. Ellison, how are you?"

Mariah seized the opportunity. "Thank you, Mrs. Wilkinson. I'm afraid we still have not found Sadie Alsop, and we fear that she might be lying somewhere ill or injured."

"Good heavens! How dreadful. And the weather is appalling! Oswald?"

"Fanny, there is far more to this than someone falling and unable to get up. They are making the charge that Sadie, poor soul, is guilty of trying to blackmail people."

"Oh, dear," she sighed. "I'm afraid that is true."

"Fanny! What . . . ?"

"I didn't tell you because you would have to ask them if the accusations are true, and they should remain private."

"She tried to blackmail you?"

"Yes."

He stared at his wife. "Surely, she was mistaken."

"She was not, Oswald. She tried it on me. I told her I would have to get the money from you, and you would want to know why. Then I insisted that you hear it directly from her. That's when she changed her mind about making good her threats. I know that other people were in different situations."

"Why didn't you tell me?" he demanded, the emotion naked in his face. "Did you think I wouldn't forgive you? What could you possibly have done that she would . . . ?" He could not complete that question. Clearly, he did not want to know the answer.

His wife's face softened. "You have the whole village's griefs and confusions, regrets and fears to deal with, my dear. I'm quite capable of dealing with this. No crime occurred. Sadie tried to blackmail me and I refused to submit. Now, it seems that some of her other victims have dealt with her threats in their own way. They had not you, my dear, to stand with them. Or at least, they thought they had not."

Wilkinson stood still for a moment, a blush of sadness that he could not hide on his face. Then he turned to Oliver. "I will go and ring the bells myself. Then when people come, I shall—"

"You'll turn to me and I'll speak to them." Oliver smiled. It changed his face from grim to charming. "I can speak as a victim, knowing what she threatened to do to me, without drawing anyone else in. We need every help we can find."

"Don't send anyone alone," Fanny instructed.

"We're going in groups of three," Mariah stated, "for everyone's safety."

The vicar and his wife glanced at each other, but no one argued.

"And we must send for Constable Hendershott," added Oliver.

"Yes, of course," the vicar agreed, and then excused himself.

Five minutes later, a carillon of bells rang out in the cold, damp air, a strange and frantic rhythm, urgent, even harsh, every village's call of alarm.

*W*hen the crowd of villagers was gathered inside the church, about sixty of them, most of them carrying lanterns and all dressed in their heaviest coats, hats, scarves, and gloves—plus their most rugged winter boots—the vicar appeared before them.

Mariah watched his face as he stood there with a certainty and determination she could not remember having seen in him before. She had expected Oliver to take that place in front of the village, but it was now clear that the vicar was accepting his responsibility.

"Thank you for coming," he called out. "There is reason to believe that Sadie Alsop is in grave danger. If it is humanly possible, we must find her, whether or not she is still alive. If she is not, then we must lay her at peace. That is, peace for her, but not peace for us. She's a woman some of us may not like, or may even be afraid of, and with cause. It is no secret that Sadie Alsop did some contemptible things to some of you, but for now, that is irrelevant. We know she was at the empty cottage in Briar Lane, but now she has disappeared and she may be hurt. This may have started as a drama of her own making, but it has escalated into something far more serious—for all of us." He drew in a deep breath. "Whether you like her or not, whether she has injured you or not, is not the issue. This is about who we are, how we behave. Do we celebrate the birth of Christ, with all the different meanings that has for us, and put off finding her until we are good and ready to look for her? Not even tomorrow, but maybe the next day?" He hesitated. "Or do we look for her now, and rest when she is found—possibly alive if we hurry and are in time."

No one spoke, but glances were exchanged.

Wilkinson looked at his wife, who nodded in reassurance.

"Who am I?" he asked. "That is the question I will have to answer tonight, at midnight, when we ring the bells and spread Christmas joy into the night sky. If we see angels, do we dare look at them? Or have we drawn a veil of darkness between ourselves and the newborn Christ? Whatever you believe of this night, and whether Sadie Alsop wronged you or not, you must look for her. I must, I know that. It is not who *she* is that sends us out to seek her, it is who *we* are."

He stood silent for a moment, then his eyes moved over the crowd. "Many of you were wronged by Sadie over mistakes or misfortunes in the past. It looks tragically as if one or more of you are at least partly to blame for her disappearance. If she dies, you will be held responsible for far more. Your mistakes are in the past. Hers are very much in the present. Some of you have reason to be afraid of her. For your safety, you will go in groups of three. Help one another. The ice is slippery. It is growing colder, and soon it will be dark. Find her, so we may celebrate Christmas this year, next year, and all future years knowing we did our best. In the name of God, we must find her!"

There were many murmurs from the crowd, but it was impossible to distinguish murmurs of agreement from those of submission to a task that was inescapable. Without saying it in so many words, the vicar left no doubt: it would be a grave sin to refuse, and only someone carrying an unforgivable guilt would dare to be seen refusing.

Mariah accepted as natural that she should go with Oliver, and by mutual consent, they chose Barton Alsop to be the third member of their team. Mariah knew he would bring an extra tension to the search: it was his wife who was in danger.

All of the teams were assigned an area, delineated by street names they all knew, and then they separated and began to search. In all, there were nineteen teams.

Mariah noticed that Gwendolyn went with John and Annabel. A shiver of anxiety brushed past her, and she dismissed it. The vicar had more wisdom than she had thought when he agreed to send teams of three. They all had secrets; most might be so trivial as to be ignored, but some not. At least no one would be alone with Sadie, if indeed they found her. And no one would risk being found alone with her body, and especially not the one who had deliberately left her to die.

Mariah shivered and quickened her step. She needed to stay close to Oliver. They walked carefully, Oliver insisting that she take his arm. She started to argue, then saw how silly that was. A fall could break bones, and truthfully, she wanted to be in more than verbal contact. She wished to be steadied in this journey that could not end well. That is, steadied both physically and emotionally. If they did not find Sadie, then that left the mystery unsolved, the guilt like a darkness settling over all of them. She did not want to imagine how Sadie had suffered: the fear, the guilt perhaps, certainly the knowledge that she was both feared and disliked. At least one person knew where she was, but who?

Mariah and Oliver walked without speaking, with Barton only two steps behind them. There was nothing to say. No one wanted to make conversation.

They looked in gardens, under bushes, in sheds and huts, even in piles of split logs ready for the fire.

Again and again, they came away disappointed.

Mariah wanted to say something encouraging to Barton, but everything that came to her mind sounded artificial, too carefully planned, and useless. He walked a little ahead of them now, and Mariah sensed he was desperately alone. She thought how long she had known him, only to speak to on occasion, to reply to things that meant nothing, merely politeness. She had even imagined, maybe led by Sadie's false sympathy, assumed to draw out the secret of her abuse, that when the doors were closed and he and Sadie were alone, he might be as brutal as her own husband had been. So wrong, so very wrong! The next time she judged hastily, she must remind herself of this, and how dangerous it was to accuse anyone without proof.

They came to the next house and knocked on the door to explain why they were searching the garden, and asked if they could look through the rooms of the house. They were greeted with sadness, anger at the situation, but no refusals.

They had been trying without the slightest success for over an hour and a half when they came to a house where they were offered hot cocoa and a slice of early Christmas cake, and the use of the lavatory.

Ten minutes later, they ventured out again, as darkness thickened and they found their footing took intense concentration. There were so many places they had yet to search. Mariah kept waiting to hear the pealing of the church bells, signaling that Sadie had been found.

Again, they chose not to speak. It was precarious, stepping on the ice, cracking in some places as near-freezing puddles were underfoot. Mariah found herself struggling to keep her balance, grateful to have Oliver's hand on her elbow to steady her. She glanced at Oliver, and he gave her a brief smile.

There was no sound but the wind through the bare branches, and that crack of ice as puddles were broken under heavy boots.

They reached the edge of the village where the bank sloped down to what was left of the stream. Someone had drained it higher up, and there was now a mere trickle from one pond to the next. A couple of houses stood a little distance away.

"There was a proper stream here, ten years ago," Barton commented unhappily. "Now there's practically nothing. You see that?" He pointed to a dilapidated hut now collapsing in on itself. "That used to be a useful little shed for all kinds of equipment."

Mariah felt her stomach clench and a hard knot in her throat stopped her from replying. No one spoke, but they all three moved toward the black shadow of the hut.

Barton sloshed through mud to reach what was left of the hut's door. With a grunt, he tried to wrench it open, but, although rotting, it was swollen with damp and held fast.

Before Mariah could speak, she heard him release something between a gasp and a cry.

As if instinctively, Oliver held her back.

There was a sound coming from within the hut. Like

177

a crazed man, Barton tore at the last barriers of the door, and it splintered into many pieces around him. He charged inside, stumbling and shouting "Sadie!" with mud flying all about them, barely visible in the failing light.

There was another sound from inside. Mariah's heart lurched and her breath stuck in her throat. Sadie was alive! She felt Oliver's hand tighten on her arm as he led her inside. The last thing they needed was another fall, an injury, someone else to carry back.

Inside, they found Barton kneeling, bent over what at first appeared to be a pile of muddy clothing.

Mariah stepped closer. Sadie was hunched over in an awkward crouch, as if not recognizing the people around her and fearful for her life.

"Can you find your way to the nearest house?" Oliver asked Mariah. "Barton and I will carry her as far as possible, at least to where there's warmth. Tell them what's happened and ask them to send someone to get the church bells ringing. We don't need any more searching, but we do need help to get Sadie to warmth and safety, and to a doctor, at least."

Before Mariah could turn to leave, Oliver called her back. "That young policeman we met in Bridgetown, Hendershott—Mrs. Wilkinson called him and he should be on his way. We'll soon know who did this."

She turned without answering and stumbled away toward the black outline of the nearest house. It was perhaps a hundred yards, but it felt far more. Several times she nearly fell in the freezing mud.

When at last she reached the front door of the house, she was past caring what she looked like. She rang the bell, and after only seconds she banged on the door itself.

It opened and a woman looked back at her, first with alarm, and then concern. "You look awful! Did you fall? Did someone—" She stopped.

"We found Sadie Alsop," Mariah gasped. "She's been missing for days. She's barely alive, down in that old shed by the stream."

"Oh, my heavens!" the woman declared. "Come inside. You look perished. I'll fetch my husband, and my son. Come in! Come!" She reached forward, as if Mariah were about to collapse. "William!" she called loudly, her voice sharp with alarm. "Come here, right now!"

Almost immediately, a burly man appeared from the back of the house in the direction of the kitchen. He stared at Mariah. "Great heavens! What has happened? Why are you—"

"They've found Sadie Alsop," his wife interrupted. "She is alive, but only just. They found her in that old shed by the stream. Go help them carry her here. We'll put her in Billy's bedroom. He can sleep on the couch. I'll send Billy to fetch the doctor."

"The doctor? He's miles away!" the man protested.

"Billy will borrow Jethro's horse," she told him. "Billy!" she called. "Come here right now!"

A broad young man came running in, eager to obey his mother, who quickly explained how he was needed.

"Yes, Mum," he said, nodding, keen to play a role in the drama.

Without asking questions, the young man threw on a heavy coat and rushed out to borrow his neighbor's horse, and then ride to the doctor's house in Bridgetown.

Within moments, the husband was also gone. He returned only minutes later, with Oliver and Barton carrying Sadie between them. They handled her gently, her body still curled over as if she were frozen into that position.

The next half hour was passed in relief, exhaustion, and anxiety. The doctor arrived and spent a great deal of time with Sadie, checking her pulse and heart often. He finally came out of the bedroom and announced that she was suffering from the cold—hypothermia, he called it, a new word to Mariah—and also exhaustion, but if he could treat her and avoid pneumonia, she might very well pull through.

Mariah and Barton took turns going in to see Sadie, each closing the door so that they could speak to her privately.

Sadie was lying with her head resting on a small pillow. She looked appalling, as if she were still in danger and might slip away, in spite of all they could do.

Mariah touched her arm and Sadie opened her eyes.

"You found me," she whispered. "I knew you would look."

"Yes, I found you," Mariah agreed. "*We* found you. Oliver, Barton, and I. But I also found out a lot I didn't know. We can talk about that later." She hesitated, wanting desperately to know the truth, but fearful she might distress the woman. Finally, she pushed her reluctance aside. "Sadie, I know you were hiding in the cottage, but who took you to that hut? Who was holding you prisoner there?"

Sadie blinked, but she did not answer.

"It was Annabel," Mariah said, answering her own question as if it were a guess, but one about which she now had little doubt. "She's the one who had the nerve to carry this through. Many people had the motive, but there was something about her, some secret only you knew and were using it against her."

Sadie looked away. It was as if, for the first time,

she had a sense of how cruel her game had been. Cruel and dangerous. "Annabel is not legally married to John Spears," she said huskily. "Her first marriage was never ended. That husband might be dead by now, but she lied to all of us, including John. Imagine if Gwendolyn had known. The sister who loved the man her own sister called her husband. Now Annabel is guilty of trying to murder me! But for you, she would have succeeded."

"She might yet!" Mariah snapped, then regretted it. This was no time to be indulging her own anger or disgust. She looked at Sadie's white face, and how she was trying to conceal the fear. She took a steadying breath. Then another. "It's over, Sadie. You can spread all the poison you like, because no one is going to pay you any longer. We all have frailties, things we would rather other people didn't know. You can't use them anymore. You are one woman against the whole village. If you have any decency in you, but also any sense of self-preservation, you will give back whatever items you've taken and hope that, in time, your victims and people of the village will forgive you."

"Somebody tried to kill me!" Sadie exclaimed with as much strength as she could muster. "You've got to—"

"No, I haven't! You must answer for the cruel things you have done. We all must answer for our sins, sooner or later. Unless we repent, really repent! You must see how ugly all of this is. Your only hope is to admit your guilt, wash it away, and where possible make amends for it."

Mariah was feeling overwhelmed by the utter cruelty and stupidity of it, all the pointless, unnecessary pain. "Make it count for something!" she told her with sudden fury. "If you want the village to forgive you, change! You can't undo the pain you've caused, the fear of having one's inner self stripped naked for all to see, their innermost sins and fears exposed. You have a long, steep hill to climb. So have we all, one way or another."

"Who are you to judge me?" Sadie demanded. "You put up with disgusting—"

"I know," said Mariah, cutting her off. "And, like a fool, I trusted you, because I thought you understood! I thought you suffered something of the same, but I was wrong. Barton is a decent man. If you choose to tell the whole village my shame, I can live with it. And I intend to. It will be yourself you cover with dirt. Is that what you want? It's going to take a lot of courage, Sadie, for you to stay here in St. Helens. But it will take even more for you to go away and be utterly alone. The nightmare will follow you. Stay here and face it. Make amends as you can, if you have the courage. And, of course, if the police let you! Blackmail is a crime, you know. Why did you do it? Were you really so short of money?"

Sadie stared at her for a long, long moment. "I was envious of the things other people had, and . . . I liked to think I had some power over them, that I was someone in the village. I wanted to be . . . important, I suppose . . ." Then, finally, the fight seeped out of her, leaving a small, pale, and frightened old woman.

Mariah felt a wave of loneliness envelope her, as if for an instant it had held them both. She put out her hand and took Sadie's. For a second there was no response. Then Sadie's fingers closed over hers in a fragile grip.

After a few seconds, there was a knock on the door. Sadie looked frightened, her hand continuing to grip Mariah's.

Mariah moved her hand away. "Come in."

Constable Hendershott entered. He was in full uniform, giving him a very official look.

Sadie stared at him as if she had seen a ghost materialize.

"Good evening, Constable," Mariah said clearly.

"I'm sorry, Mrs. Ellison," the constable replied. "I should have taken you more seriously. I'm very glad Mrs. Alsop is still alive."

"They tried to murder me!" Sadie cried, her anger and indignation almost choking her.

Constable Hendershott looked at her, contempt clear in his face. "Yes, madam, I know that. No one imagines you went to a freezing hut, by a stream, and in this weather by your own choice."

"Are you going to . . ." Sadie's voice faded away.

"Yes, ma'am. The person responsible will be arrested and charged with kidnapping, and possibly attempted murder. I'm not the one to decide that. From what I know, they probably felt that they had a reason for doing this to you, and I dare say there are plenty of people in St. Helens who will testify to that, starting with Mrs. Ellison here."

The silence was almost palpable in the room, like the presence of another being.

Sadie turned a fraction to face Mariah.

Mariah forced herself not to look away. "You must help yourself, Sadie. I can't do it for you. Blackmail is a crime, too. It is a slow, cruel torturer of people. You watched their hurt, and you did so without mercy. It's not up to me whether I will forgive you. You didn't try it on me, but I have no doubt that you were prepared to."

"But I . . ." Sadie began, and then fell silent, as if at last she understood the seriousness of her crimes.

"You have to find your own way back," Mariah told her, gentler this time. "I don't know whether anyone will charge you or not. That's up to them, and perhaps you."

In the distance the church bells rang out once, this time calling the village to prayer. It was nearly Christmas.

"I'm going to church," Mariah announced. "And I'm going to live here. I intend to buy that cottage that is for sale, where you hid out. I'm sure you know it very well. But tonight, I'm going to church with everybody else. You can't come because you are too ill. And you need time to recover, not only in body but in spirit. Then you must decide if you are for us, or not. It's a turn in the road. You choose which way you go. That's what church is really for: the chance to choose which way to go." She removed her hand from Sadie's and turned toward the door.

Mariah found Oliver standing in the hall, just outside the door. He was still wearing his heavy winter coat and hat, ready to walk into the freezing air.

"I'll take you to church," he offered.

Mariah smiled. Were the bells ringing again, or was she imagining it? It did not matter, because their music was inside her head. Loud, joyous bells of a new beginning.

She went back into the room where Sadie lay. "I'm going with Oliver. When you are well, you can attend services, too. If you so choose and, of course, if the village chooses to forgive you. They might, for their own sakes. Not to silence you—you have no more power to hurt them—but because they believe in mercy . . . and hope."

Before Sadie could respond, Mariah turned away, took Oliver's arm, and left the house.

When they were on the street, arm in arm, and surrounded by the sharp, freezing air, she turned to him. "What about Annabel?" Mariah revealed Annabel as Sadie's kidnapper but said nothing about her marriage not being legal. As the facts became known, he would learn this soon enough. "Sadie knew something very damaging. I wonder how she discovered it."

"Sadie's a good detective," Oliver replied. "One slip of a remark, followed up diligently, and over the years a lot of secrets can be traced back to the beginning. Sadie could feign friendship very well. I don't know how many other people's secrets she knew, and I don't want to find out. Dealing with mistakes, repaying old debts, all of that should be a private thing. All we are required to do is forgive others. Unless the law is broken. And I'm afraid Annabel will have to answer to the law. As Sadie's kidnapper, and someone who nearly caused her death—and Sadie would have died, had we not found her—Annabel will pay that price. It's up to the police. When John is told the truth about everything she has done, I doubt he'll forgive her."

Mariah was torn. She wanted to share what she knew with Oliver, but did that make her a gossip? She finally made the decision. When she told him about the bigamy, he said nothing. He shook his head, as if finding this hard to believe. "It's almost worse than attempted murder," said Mariah. Then a little smile played across her mouth.

"What?" Oliver said, seeing it. "Tell me!"

"I shouldn't, but if John is legally free, perhaps he will choose the right sister this time."

Oliver smiled a little wryly. "That depends, of course, on whether or not Gwendolyn will have him."

Mariah said nothing, but her heart gave a little lurch of happiness at the thought.

Oliver took her arm more tightly. It was pitch dark and they were walking slowly, feeling their way rather than seeing it. The streetlamps were lit, but there were dark places in the spaces between. It was later than she had thought.

As Mariah and Oliver approached the church, John Spears and Gwendolyn walked by them, nodding their greetings, and stepped inside. The looks exchanged among all of them conveyed the shared knowledge of pain, fear, loneliness deep inside, and perhaps the beginning of new lives.

Oliver broke the silence. "Are you really going to buy that cottage?" There was more than curiosity in his voice. There was emotion, too, as if her answer mattered to him.

She had no doubt at all. "Yes, I am."

For a second there was no sound but the crackle of ice as Mariah trod on another frozen puddle. "Good," he said quietly. "Very good."

They stepped into the church and took their seats. There was a low murmur, and Mariah guessed that information about Sadie's rescue and Annabel's arrest was being shared.

Suddenly, all sounds stopped and heads began to turn. Mariah and Oliver also looked back to see who had entered.

Walking down the aisle was Dorothy, head high, best hat on. Holding her hand, her eyes wide with wonder, was a little girl, Jenny.

At first, the people stared at them, and then they smiled. A few reached out to touch Dorothy's arm.

A young man moved to make room for both of them,

and then handed Dorothy a hymn book. She took it hesitantly. In a gesture that struck Mariah as the height of kindness, he handed his own hymn book to little Jenny. She took it, smiling, and held it with both hands, as if it were something precious. He smiled back.

People throughout the church nodded their silent approval. Even more, their understanding and compassion.

Mariah found herself smiling with the joy of it. The joy was made even greater when Oliver tightened his arm around her and pulled her close.

Suddenly, the air was filled with the sound of bells. Not to call the townspeople together in an emergency, nor to announce the discovery of a missing woman who had brought fear and grief to this village. This time, peal after peal announced that it was Christmas.

ABOUT THE AUTHOR

ANNE PERRY was the bestselling author of two acclaimed series set in Victorian England: the William Monk novels and the Charlotte and Thomas Pitt novels. She was also the author of a series featuring Charlotte and Thomas Pitt's son, Daniel, as well as the Elena Standish series; a series of five World War I novels; twenty-one holiday novels; and a historical novel, *The Sheen on the Silk,* set in the Byzantine Empire. Anne Perry died in 2023.

anneperry.us

ABOUT THE TYPE

This book was set in Century Schoolbook, a member of the Century family of typefaces. It was designed in the 1890s by Theodore Low De Vinne (1828–1914) of the American Type Founders Company, in collaboration with Linn Boyd Benton (1844–1932). It was one of the earliest types designed for a specific purpose, the *Century* magazine, because it was able to maintain the economies of a narrower typeface while using stronger serifs and thickened verticals.